I0700165

muse

a novella
by LCW Allingham

Speculation Publications

To my mom.

Who loved this book because she knew
her muses so well.

Thank you for being my first reader for so
many years. Thank you for teaching me
art and filling my world with creativity.

Your muses miss you, Mom.

And so do I.

This book contains profanity, sex,
abuse, violence, death, suicide, sexual
assault, and blood & gore

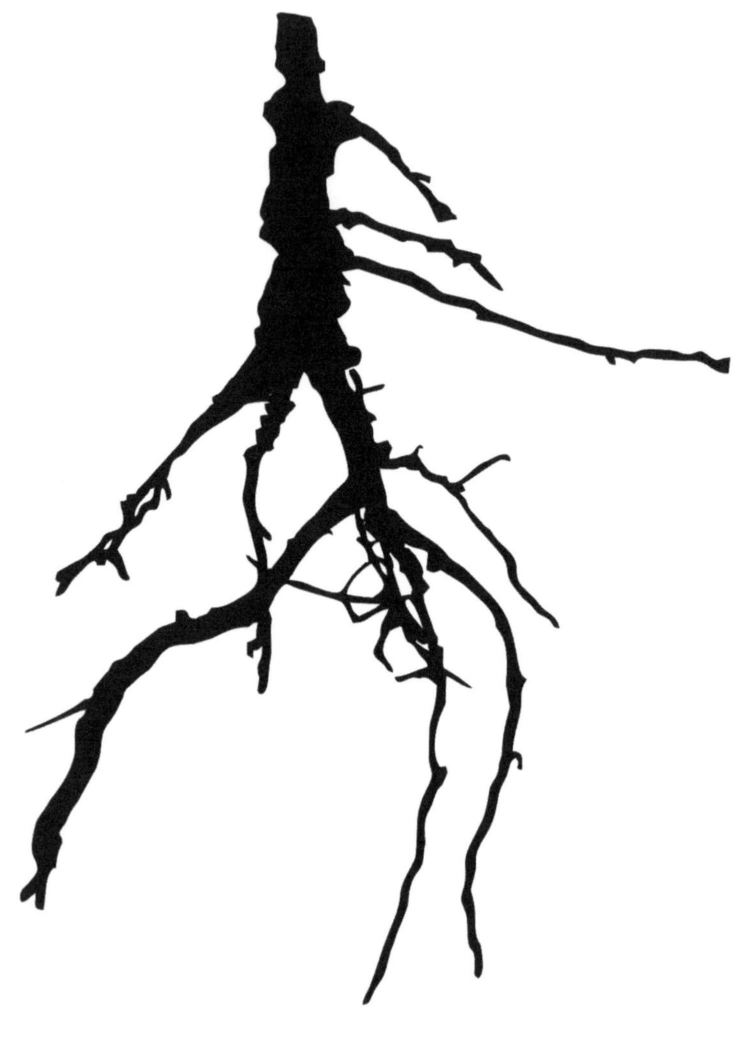

1

"Glonciel is done. Dried up."

Mr. Black tapped the tips of his long fingers together at the head of the mahogany table. "She hasn't painted so much as a dandelion since last May."

"She may still have something left in her," Mr. Green said. "She was talking about sunflowers when I spoke with her last night."

The paneled room was kept dim, the tall windows blocked by thick velvet drapes. Narrow red tapered candles from the grand chandelier provided flickering light.

"She's done," agreed Mr. Silver. The candlelight caught streaks of gold in his dark blond hair. "Cut her off."

"So is Jackson," said Mr. Black. "The next exhibition will be his last."

"Malik Jackson said he's working on an entirely new concept." Mr. Green pinched his thin lips together and worked his thumbnail underneath the table, where it found the familiar dent he had created over the years.

"If he doesn't produce in a month, he's no good to us," Mr. Silver said.

"We'll wait and see how he does." Mr. Black drummed his long fingers on the table to indicate the decision was made, although his associates had not yet agreed.

"Fleck is still going strong," Mr. Green suggested. "I previewed his new pastel collection last week. It's magnificent."

"Not magnificent enough." Mr. Silver shook his head. "I'm disappointed with Fleck. He seemed like he was going to be a long haul."

"When was the last time we found a long haul?" Mr. Black frowned, the lines around his mouth folding into deep creases that hinted at his age.

"Too long," said Mr. Silver.

"If you would only give them a chance…" Mr. Green started, but under the glare of his associates, he withered into his seat.

"More talent then," said Mr. Black. "Better talent."

"Better and bankable," agreed Mr. Silver.

"Cedric Fleck has only started!" said Mr. Green, his gray eyes shining with what could be mistaken as tears.

"He's going down fast," said Mr. Black.

"Too fast," said Mr. Silver.

"He's still got a spark left in him," Mr. Black added, his lip curling slightly as if he was practicing his smoldering looks right at the table. "But the way he goes, it won't be long. Find someone new."

"Something fresh."

"Something powerful."

Mr. Green stood abruptly, taking a minute to adjust the lapels of his bespoke Italian suit coat before stalking out of the dark conference room.

After the slamming door indicated Mr. Green had left the Manhattan brownstone, Mr. Silver yawned and leaned back in his chair. "He's too sensitive."

"He always has been," Mr. Black said. "But he is the best."

"Oh, no doubt. No doubt. Still, I wonder if he won't become a problem."

"If he does, we will address it," Mr. Black said. "We thrive and fall together. And Mr. Green very much wants to thrive."

The net was cast wide. Miami, Kansas City, country clubs and youth groups, each whisper examined, cataloged and thrown back to sea. Mr. Green would know when he found his white whale, but until he did, he traveled, through sticky stops and sweltering stations, packed in with the sweating masses slogging through their art-starved lives. He rested each night in five-star hotels, with forty-dollar martinis and Egyptian cotton sheets. He moved through the faceless swarms waiting for a tug on the line.

Mr. Green dozed in a bus station, wavering on an old dream of the French countryside, the taste of mud in his mouth, the stench of marsh in his nostrils, when the line went live. The sudden jolt was so hard and sharp it nearly yanked him from his tacky plastic chair. A buzz ran up his legs, and his dream faded immediately as his senses filled with the clean, green scent of spring in early bloom.

"—that old bastard welder I work with," a neo-hipster punk in a bus terminal said into his phone. "No, the one who's always carting around the art supplies. Dude lives in a double-wide in Park Flatts, jacked as shit, but he's over at the craft store on his lunch break…Naw, he says it's for his neighbor."

When the young man got off his phone, Mr. Green leaned back, smiling disarmingly. "Excuse me, Sir, I didn't mean to eavesdrop, but I couldn't help overhear something you said. You see, I'm an art agent."

He reached into his suit and pulled out a business card and a fifty-dollar bill.

A traded bus ticket, another odorous ride, then a cab to a mud pit in the middle of the sticks. The line got brighter the closer he came, the promise of ripe fruit like a lure shining just below the surface of a lake. Mr. Green's net closed, and he pulled it in, finding himself at the dirty, dented door of the ancient modular home of Miss Terra Desmarais.

Cedric Fleck took a deep hit and sank back into Bernard Black's lap. "What is in this shit?" he giggled, his insides tickling beautifully as the exposed beams of his new studio apartment spun into kaleidoscope shapes.

"Does it matter?" Bernard took a hit of his own and stroked Cedric's clammy forehead. Cedric gazed up at Bernard's mature, chiseled face, trying to find the pupils in his dark eyes. Sometimes Cedric convinced himself they weren't there at all, as if he were gazing upon the face of a god. He was the most beautiful man Cedric had ever seen, all tall, dark and handsome with the mystery to go along with it.

Bernard blew a plume of pungent smoke into his face. Cedric smiled and rolled up to take another hit. This was their communion, he and Bernard. They would get high as hell and make love. Then Cedric would draw for hours.

He was inspired. He thought it was his best work. Bernard recently suggested that Cedric was losing his touch, but he would see. When the next collection came out, he would see how Cedric's love translated to paper. Cedric had a special piece he'd already set aside for the art critic who kept his bed warm.

"Sheena Meegan called today about taking my *Unearthed* exhibit at the Pavilion," Cedric said. "She's talking about a tour if it does well."

"Sheena Meegan is a hack." Bernard took a long hit and blew the smoke into lazy rings.

"I've liked the exhibits she's done in the last year. She had Dana Glonciel—"

"Glonciel is done. And if I was being too subtle, I meant to say Sheena is a bed-climbing wannabe with no vision. Ignore her. She's not worth you."

Cedric sniffed, stung. Bernard was the industry pro, the one who knew everything. Still, Cedric wasn't so new to this, and it wasn't like Bernard was his agent. Cedric liked Dana Glonciel's work, and he liked Sheena Meegan. She understood what Cedric was doing. Better than Bernard sometimes.

He didn't say anything. Bernard was wearing a fitted gray button-down shirt, and every time he lifted the hookah pipe his muscles rippled beneath it. Besides, Bernard had made his career. Cedric had been killing himself working on the streets, living out of his sister's old Ford Escort, choosing between art supplies and food, before he got a show in a tiny no-name Brooklyn gallery that Bernard Black, international art critic and kingmaker, just happened to stroll into.

Now Cedric was making real money, and people came from all over the country to buy his work. He had everything he ever wanted.

Except Bernard.

Whenever they started to get close, Bernard pushed Cedric back to arm's length.

Cedric would think they were getting serious, and then he'd see pictures of Bernard with one of his many pretty girls or boys on Sheena Meegan's social media. He couldn't expect a guy as hot and worldly as Bernard to commit to only him, but still…

"Do you want to take this to bed?" Cedric asked, massaging Bernard's shoulder.

"Not tonight, I'm afraid. I have to go to an exhibit in an hour. Some daft bitch is standing naked and letting people write on her with Sharpies. It's going to be painfully boring, but I have to have something to write up tomorrow."

Cedric frowned. "Just a quick one?"

"Sorry." Bernard lifted his brows and lips at the same time, yet his expression remained blank, cold, his black eyes flat. He stood up and the hookah went out at the same time. "Try to get some work done, though. You really want to shine at this next exhibit. It's going to be an important one."

So they were back here again. Cedric wasn't sure what he'd done wrong. Everything had been going so well. He hadn't made any demands of Bernard. His work was coming along great, and he thought the amazing hybrid pot was a sign of a good night.

Cedric stood up and leaned in for a kiss. Bernard planted one on his cheek and walked out of the loft.

Never enough. "Cedric the Sometimes." His heart pounded so hard it hurt while he tried to keep his face impassive, his eyes dry. If Bernard didn't want him, why did he even come over? Cedric was absolutely certain if Bernard had not called, he would feel a hundred times better right now.

He poured himself a strong drink and threw it back. Then he poured another and took it to his studio, where he coated a colorful landscape in progress with black and gray pastel.

Two trailers in Park Flatts had somehow shifted closer to each other over the years. One belonged to Jim Megus, a middle-aged second-shift welder and the meanest old bastard anyone had ever met. The other was occupied by a skinny girl with dishwater-colored hair and big black eyes so damned unsettling that all her neighbors went out of their way to avoid her stare. Her name was Terra Desmarais, but her neighbors called her the Flatts Witch.

These two villains of the trailer park seemed to get along well with each other. Sometimes Jim left a bag of groceries on the step of the girl's narrow modular, and sometimes the girl left bottles of Old Grandad on the steps of Jim's double wide.

As their trailers got closer together, folks surmised through shifting ground in the muddy seasons, the witch and the bastard were seen around town together, or sitting together in their lawn chairs. Talking, never loud, unless some poor kid happened too close to Jim's property, which was specified with bright orange traffic cones and spray paint. Then Jim was likely to start cussing and throwing rocks.

No one had ever heard the witch speak, but it seemed she talked to Jim. And it seemed Jim talked about her, to somebody, somewhere, about what it was that she did inside her trailer.

When Mr. Green showed up at the door of Terra Desmarais's modular, she let him in. After all, he was a swanky man wearing a suit and shiny shoes flecked with trailer park mud and she was just…Terra, the Flatts Witch, a shut in, with no job and only one friend.

"I think there's some sorta confusion here, Sir," she said. "I don't got nothing you would be looking to be buying."

Mr. Green brushed past her, and saw that she was lying. Terra Desmarais's trailer was cluttered with paintings. Paintings like he had never seen in his long life. Cheap, craft-store temperas that were so vivid and so unique that he froze midstride, gazing upon their glory.

Miss Desmarais worked in abstract, such beautiful compositions that he nearly cried, right there in her trailer. There were colors he'd never seen before. Structures he'd never dreamed of. Each piece a poem, a song, a wretched and rejoicing movement of life. His heart lifted and plummeted with the butterfly queasiness of a roller coaster and it took a while for him to realize that Terra was talking.

"Where did you study?" He cut off whatever she'd been saying.

"That's what I'm telling you!" She sighed. "This ain't nothing. I just started doing it one day. I didn't learn from nobody or nothing. I just like to do it. For myself. I never even tried to sell this shit."

"Well, you are going to," Mr. Green said, pulling out his business card—perfect black embossed print on heavy snow-white linen paper—and handing it to her. "Garret Green, art agent. Would it be okay if I took a few photos of your work?"

"I, um, I guess so?" Terra shrugged and shifted her weight. She wore a stained gray tank top and a pair of dirty cutoff shorts—real cutoffs, not store bought—and real dirty, not fashionably discolored. They were too big on her, and her skinny legs jutted out from the bottom like two popsicle sticks with scabby knees.

"Brilliant." He spun his camera around the room, clicking rapid fire.

"Why do you need to take pictures?"

"I want to send them to some associates of mine," Mr. Green said. "Miss Desmarais, you say you never studied anywhere?"

"I just like to paint," she said. "People think it's weird."

"It is weird." Mr. Green smiled wide. "It's…it's…it's wonderful. All your work is wonderful. Have you ever thought of putting it in a gallery?"

"I just—I just like to paint it. I ain't trying to be something I'm not." Terra's tone was exasperated.

"I assure you, Miss Desmarais, you are something I have never seen before. And that is saying something. If I offered you a ticket to New York City, would you come and bring your artwork? We…*I* would pay all your expenses."

"You mean, like, for real? Like not some kinda a scam?"

"Surely not. I can provide you with documentation all the way."

"Could I bring Jim? He's sorta my…I dunno, like, he's never left this place, and I would feel bad if I didn't take him."

"Yes. You and Jim. Excellent. I will send a curator here to pack your work."

"All of it?"

"Certainly. It will still be yours, but it will be in New York, where people will buy it. And I will get about finding you a patron to put you up in a nice place while you stay in the city. In the meantime, you'll stay at my flat, um, apartment in Soho. I don't live there, so you can have it for a while. How does that sound?"

"A patron?"

"Someone who appreciates your work and will cover your expenses."

"Well, I don't need much." Terra shook her head.

She was such an odd-looking girl. Impossible to put an age on. As dingy and common as her trailer park, yet somehow disquieting, evocative, like her paintings. It was no wonder that people avoided her, but the power of her art…Mr. Green was giddy with the potential in the trailer.

Raw talent. Undiscovered and ignorant. He had found her, and she would be his. Not Black's. Not Silver's. He would take this one and keep her until he was sure she could withstand their greedy needs.

Dana Glonciel felt sick, run down, and tired as Scott Silver fucked her from behind. It felt like he had been at it forever, but she was having a hard time concentrating. That coke she'd snorted before they went at it wasn't helping. What she really needed was sleep. For a week. As she started to nod off, Scott grabbed her hair and yanked her neck back. She winced but didn't cry out.

"Am I boring you?" he asked.

"No, baby," she said, automatically.

He kept his hand tangled in her hair, pulling enough for it to hurt. He'd done so much for her; she could at least pretend she was enjoying this. His other fingers dug into her thigh so hard she was sure to have bruises again. Dana tried to think back to when they'd started sleeping together, a few years ago. It had been good then. Scott wasn't the best of her lovers, but it hadn't hurt. When had he gotten so rough?

He finally finished, smacking her so hard on the ass that she yelped. He pushed her down into the bed. She rolled onto her back and smiled at him; her eyes heavy.

"I forgot to mention, I'm throwing you a dinner party at the townhouse, with some friends," Scott said. "Tomorrow night."

"Anyone I know?"

"Of course. You know exactly who."

Dana's heart drummed in her chest, but she wasn't sure if it was excitement or fear. Scott Silver had powerful friends. They used to all party together a lot, but recently no one was returning her calls.

She had to get to work. She knew she had to get to work. Nothing new for almost a year, although she'd lied and told everyone that she had completed the *Blossoms of Youth* collection a few months ago.

But she was so damned tired, and there was never time to sleep. If it wasn't a party, or an interview, or an opening, or a consultation, it was Scott, and she owed Scott. He had made it possible for her to live in New York when she was starting out. Scott was a great guy, a *great* guy. Ambitious, smart as hell, and with an eye for art. He knew everyone, and he introduced Dana to all of them.

When he was with his "friends," he was different. They all were different when they were together. Things got out of hand sometimes. Dana would do stuff she didn't normally do, stuff she wasn't proud of. New York and success had changed her. When she really thought about it, Scott and his friends had helped coordinate those changes.

"I don't know," she said. "I really need to spend a few days resting up, so I can get to work on my next collection. I have this idea…"

She didn't finish the thought. She didn't have an idea. None at all, for a solid year. She was selling off her old pieces, her name still meant something, but if she didn't start producing new art, all of this would go.

She'd only be left with the changes.

"Really? You want to pass up an opportunity now?" Scott lit up a cigarette and walked into the living room of his penthouse, naked. He wasn't in as good of shape as he had been. He looked like he'd been indulging too much recently. A tight pad of fat hung from his belly that hadn't been there when they started sleeping together. His ass was thicker and jiggly, but Scott wore it like he earned it, and she supposed he had. Other women probably found it hot, but it made Dana feel violated in some way she didn't understand.

She had no business judging. She'd been losing weight so fast that she'd be invisible in a few months.

She remained on his bed, eyes closed, willing herself to sleep, but his words rattled around in her head. She couldn't pass up the chance to spend the evening with Scott's friends, even if she wanted to. She needed them. If she didn't produce, they were the ones who were going to keep her afloat until she figured out her next move.

"Tomorrow night." Scott pinched her breast just as she dozed off. She opened her eyes to see him looking down at her. The way the dim bedroom light hit his face; it looked as if a dark vein throbbed from his eye to his lips. He looked feral, hungry, and the sight of him made Dana shiver.

A week after Mr. Green sent the pictures to his associates, every gallery in New York was whispering about Terra Desmarais. The partners wasted no time preparing a fertile environment for their future star.

"Have you seen her work in person yet?" Sheena Meegan asked Mr. Black when he stopped by her most recent exhibit.

"Not yet. I think her agent is anxious about letting go of his baby." Mr. Black smiled and Sheena swooned. Everyone thought Bernard Black was gorgeous, and he knew exactly when and where to take advantage of that.

Mr. Silver murmured to an art dealer, "I guess it remains to be seen if it's anything more than some lucky paint pours. It would be rather surprising for the work to live up to the hype."

"Says the man who's invested in all the best artists in the city," the dealer laughed.

Mr. Silver shrugged as if it were inconsequential.

The men both spoke about it at every event they attended, joking about how they had not yet seen the work, suggesting it was unlikely to come to anything, but they had people talking. Mr. Green was so confident about this artist, he insisted she start out big. No "accidental discoveries" this time. Terra Desmarais had already been an accidental discovery. Now she was coming to New York as the Next Big Thing, under a roaring buzz of secrecy.

It infuriated Mr. Black and Mr. Silver.

"Why the games?" Mr. Black asked Mr. Green as soon as he arrived at Mr. Silver's Park Avenue limestone townhouse for dinner. Silver owned many properties, a Tribecca loft for selling art, a Midtown East apartment for flings, but he preferred the three story town-home for artist parties. It was close to their fifth avenue brownstone, in case they ran into any trouble. "Where is the collection?"

"I'm having it all mounted and framed." Mr. Green tossed his coat on the Victorian hall tree and poured himself a scotch. "I told you, it's very cheap material. It needs to be handled carefully if it's going to be worth anything."

"If what you say about it is true, it's going to be worth plenty whether it's in good shape or not. When can we see it?"

"After I secure the opening."

"No." Mr. Silver walked out of his bedroom. He wore a meticulously tailored La Belle Epoque suit with a long tail and satin lapels, and he struggled to fasten the cummerbund around his thickening waist. "That is unacceptable, Green. I am not financing anyone until I see their work."

"So, wait until you see her work to finance her." Mr. Green waved his hand.

Mr. Black and Mr. Silver exchanged looks. "There is a formula we follow, Garret," Mr. Black said, his voice low and gravelly.

"She isn't comfortable with a patron yet," Mr. Green said. "She's…shy. Doesn't have a sense of her worth."

He smiled at the thought of her, and Mr. Black and Mr. Silver shared another look.

"Let me show her what she can accomplish." Mr. Green's indifferent tone made his associates very uneasy. "Then she will open up. Don't worry. I have this handled. Do you trust my taste or not?" Mr. Black and Mr. Silver hated Green's smugness, but there was nothing they could do. This was his department, and he was the best.

The doorbell rang and Mr. Silver sighed. "Well, at least we'll be done with this washed-up pile of garbage."

He opened the door. Their dinner guest walked in, a bit shaky on her high designer heels, pale in the face with dark circles under her eyes.

"Dana, darling, how nice of you to join us." Mr. Silver embraced her.

Dana Glonciel kissed his cheeks and cast a worried look over at Mr. Black. Then she saw Mr. Green.

"I was wondering if you would be here, Garret," she said. "You haven't called me back in weeks." She didn't sound angry, only defeated.

Mr. Green took her hand. "I am sorry, Dana. I just signed a new client, and I've been rather busy."

"I heard," Dana said. "Is she really as good as people are saying? I'd love to see her work."

Mr. Green patted her hand. "I hope you get the chance," he said.

Mr. Green stopped by the apartment a week after Terra arrived in New York and was greeted by the hulking slob of a man Terra called Jim.

"Is Ms. Desmarais in?" Mr. Green asked.

Jim's glare was openly hostile, but he walked back into the apartment and left the door open. Mr. Green watched him enter the master bedroom, which he'd had meticulously furnished for Terra. Terra walked out of the guest bedroom a moment later with a paint smudge across her face.

"Hi, Garret," she said. "Y'all want to stay for dinner? We're having pulled pork. Jim makes it up real good."

"No, thank you," Mr. Green replied. He had dinner reservations with Sheena Meegan at Nourriture Aérienne and no desire for whatever pulled pork was.

"I merely stopped by to see how you're settling in. I see you are using the supplies I got you." Mr. Green counted at least six new pieces leaned up against the paint-spattered brick walls of the living room. Two oils, an ink, a watercolor, a pastel, and a charcoal. Most artists had a preferred medium, but Terra seemed to excel in them all.

"Yeah, I dunno," Terra wandered into the kitchen to wash palettes in the farmhouse sink.

Mr. Green stopped in front of the canvas she was working on. It was a large acrylic, full of golds and whites, like a sunburst, but with a black shadow passing over top of it and tendrils reaching out from the shadow.

His heart sped up and something expanded in his chest, sending warm tingles through his body. He was five and Opa was waiting for him and they still had a year before he was gone. He was running as fast as his legs could go.

"An eclipse," he said through his breath as Terra came back into the room. "This is brilliant. Do you think you'll have it done in time for the show?"

"Yeah, I'll probably finish it today," Terra said. "I dunno. I was just fooling around with it."

"It's really…something." Mr. Green had a hard time catching his breath. The hues of yellow and gold were so startling it felt as if he was looking directly into the sun. "Can I—"

He stopped himself. He was treading into dangerous ground.

"What?" Terra asked, chewing nervously on the inside of her cheek. She looked strangely beautiful today, with her mud-colored hair tied back in a messy knot, a smudge of paint along the curve of her nostril and her black eyes sparkling in the natural light of the apartment.

"Can I watch you work? For a bit?"

She shrugged her skinny shoulders. "I guess."

"Are you sure?" he asked, feeling almost shy about it.

"I mean, I dunno. I don't mind or nothing. But, like, I don't talk when I'm working. Jim just stays in his room and watches TV 'cause he knows I won't hear him if he says anything."

"That is fine," Mr. Green said. "I won't say a word."

Terra worried her lip. "All right."

Mr. Green sat carefully on the blue velvet camelback sofa, and Terra picked up her palette, which she'd wrapped in cheap plastic wrap to keep from drying out. She grabbed a palette knife and placed the end of a thick brush in her mouth. For a moment she considered the painting, tilting her head from side to side. Then she started to scrape the knife through her paints, cutting them into new shades and smearing them onto the canvas.

Mr. Green felt as if he were watching his child be born. The air seemed to fill with a beautiful glowing warmth that flowed through him and out of him, and all of it emanated from Terra Desmarais. She was a master, and he was witnessing the birth of a masterpiece.

"Why the fuck are you looking at her like that? You look like some kinda perv." Jim stood in the doorway to the master bedroom. "You gonna start jacking off in a minute?"

"I—" Mr. Green was startled from the spell by the big man's abrasive voice.

"You think you're smart," Jim said. "You think I don't see what you're doing, but I know. I'm not falling for any of your bullshit. And I have her back, all the time."

"That's very good of you, Sir," Mr. Green replied, a bit shaken.

Terra didn't even seem to realize they were both there in the room, having a rather hostile conversation. Mr. Green pressed. "I am glad Terra has someone to take care of her. I hope you aren't taking advantage of her hospitality."

Jim rolled his thick shoulders, his bulk shifting around his barrel chest. "We'll see who's taking advantage, *Mr. Green*." He spoke the name like it was a joke.

Mr. Green felt an uncomfortable coiling, somewhere deep inside of him.

There's a song like angels and cold hands on her skin. A push and pull, and she is at their whims, unable to speak or move for herself. Their little doll. Their wind-up toy. Pull the lever and watch her work.

She has been such an eager little beaver in their designer clothes, her face on billboards, her paint in print, and here she is on her knees again saying please please please give me another chance.

It hurts now. It didn't hurt before, when she had padding, when she had a core, but now it's only hollow spaces and no amount of cum or blow is going to fill them up anymore.

They're laughing like it's funny, and she can see them well for the first time. Their faces drip and shift and each time they reach for her, the tendrils slide in through her pores, push and pull and sucking her in, while they lick the drugs off her bare skin.

You wanted this, they say. You asked for this.

And she nods her head like it's true. She's still on her knees and she's still asking for more, but there's nothing more to give.

These men of mud have sucked her dry.

Oh, but when she finally realizes that they're not angels singing, but sirens, then there's a moment of clarity, and a light in the distance, cutting through the fog.

There is redemption, somewhere. She can feel it calling.

Eclipse was the centerpiece of the entire display, set at the far end of the gallery but in view as soon as guests walked into the door. Mr. Green had hired three experts to work with Sheena to lay out the exhibit but had fired all of them and let Terra hang things where she wanted. She had a good eye for that too.

As soon as Mr. Black and Mr. Silver walked in for a special early preview, their faces lit up. Their cynicism, perhaps for the first time ever, lifted away into awe.

"Is she here?" Mr. Black asked.

"She is finishing another piece," Mr. Green explained. "She'll be at the opening tomorrow night."

"So, we have to meet her with everyone else?" Mr. Silver cried. "Unacceptable."

"I brought the dress that she should wear." Mr. Black shoved a glossy black box at Mr. Green. "And she has an appointment at Bacall's for hair and makeup for tomorrow."

"I'll tell her, but she might…"

He realized he was arguing with no one. Black and Silver had already floated away from him, transfixed by the work on the walls of the mid-sized gallery that Silver had chosen to make his Next Best Thing.

"It's brilliant," Mr. Black muttered. "Absolutely perfect."

"Gorgeous," Mr. Silver hissed from the other side of the gallery. "Just gorgeous."

Mr. Green settled back onto a leather sofa at the edge of the gallery. He tried to let the astonished praise fill him, but his stomach was unsettled. He tried to imagine introducing Terra to Mr. Black and Mr. Silver at the opening tomorrow, like he had introduced Dana, and Malik, and Cedric. Like he had introduced Vincent and Francisco and Georgia.

None of them had lived up to their full potential.

But Mr. Green was learning his lesson at last. Terra was a gift. An angel, and he would not let his associates drain her before she produced her best work. They had been greedy with Dana, hungry and eager to ignore the rules.

"Not with Terra," he whispered to himself.

8

"I look stupid," Terra said through the closed door of her bedroom, while Jim waited on the velvet sofa in the shabbiest suit Mr. Green had ever seen. Faded, rust-colored corduroy with stained elbow patches over a gray dollar-store button-down shirt. Mr. Green had offered to buy him one or even lend him one if Jim was feeling particularly noble about money (in spite of living in the master suite rent free) but Jim just made a horrific grunting-snorting sound to clear his throat.

"I'm sure you look lovely," Mr. Green called back. "The dress is a Joel Vanache. It's one of a kind."

Terra pushed open her bedroom door, her mouth twisted up on one side. She was not a vision. She was absolutely right. The dress, designed exactly for women of her slender size and skinny limbs, hung on her in all of the wrong ways.

"You look like a little girl in her mama's dress," Jim said from the couch and cracked open a beer. He wasn't wrong. The jet-black A-line cocktail dress was supposed to look elegant, but it gapped at her chest, flopped over her hips and seemed to bunch around her knees.

"It's okay," Mr. Green said. "We have a few hours before the opening. We can go shopping. Try on some new dresses."

"All this stuff is too swanky for me," Terra said. "Why can't I go like myself?"

Mr. Green winced. Braless in a stained tank top and too-large cutoff shorts was not going to fly for a premiere. It could potentially derail the entire exhibit, and Mr. Green could only imagine the fit his associates would throw.

Something had to be done, and Terra was right. A "swanky" dress truly wasn't her. Mr. Black was going to be mad. He enjoyed a certain prestige through his cross promotions, noting the designers that up-and-coming artists wore, the musicians they favored, the restaurants where they ate. It had served him quite well over the years.

It wasn't going to tonight. "All right, let's see what is in your closet," Mr. Green said.

Cedric tried to stay close to Bernard, but the critic kept melting into the shadows between the vivid paintings. It was his work, Cedric knew, but they hadn't been together for weeks. The neglect and fear of impending rejection made him feel uncomfortably dour and insecure.

Add to that, all this fuss over some hick with a paintbrush. The press knew nothing about her, but for some reason they all had to come out to see her debut.

Her work was quite something, Cedric had to admit. Her colors made him feel…almost…well *something*. Something he couldn't quite figure out.

"Are you enjoying the show, Mr. Fleck?" a voice at his shoulder asked. He turned to see Scott Silver's haughty smirk. Scott leaned against the wall beside a brilliant green canvas that vaguely resembled …something…something Cedric felt deep in his bones.

What the hell was this artist smoking, and where could he get some?

"It's unique," Cedric said.

Scott patted him on the back. "Unique," he echoed. "That's what I thought. Unique. The girl has talent. Surprising for a muddy smudge of trailer trash."

Cedric didn't like the look in Scott's eyes. The vibrant colors of the painting, and the bright white of the lights, glinted off them and made them look unnatural and hungry. He felt an uncomfortable weight in his diaphragm. A familiar unsettling that had been catching up with him more and more recently.

He smiled and nodded at Scott because he had to. Scott had financed him when he had nothing. He gave him the means to pursue his art full time, with all the materials and space he needed, without scrambling to work three jobs.

Scott knew Cedric was just a smudge of trash too. Not from a trailer, but close enough. Maybe even worse. Garret Green had found Cedric scribbling chalk drawings in a tattered notebook, outside of an underground club where Cedric worked—any job available—to make enough for art supplies, gas, and his membership at a cheap gym where he could shower. He was living off whatever food and drugs the patrons left at their tables when the club closed. He was barely surviving on the streets.

Cedric grappled with whether he should say something, suddenly defensive of this very woman he'd been mentally criticizing moments before.

Scott's eyes drifted past him and narrowed. "Shit."

Cedric followed his glare and saw a homeless woman staggering into the gallery. The considerable crowd of art elites gave her a wide berth, snapping pictures on their phones and chattering excitedly about the oddity as the woman gazed about the room. Her eyes landed on Scott. She waved enthusiastically, her grime-smeared face lifting into a smile as she swayed toward them.

Bernard appeared next to Cedric and took his arm. "Let's get some fresh air," he said. He pulled Cedric toward the back of the gallery as the woman stumbled toward them.

"Scott, Scott, this is a lovely exhibit, isn't it?" she slurred. As she drew close, Cedric realized that the rags she wore was actually couture soaked in filth.

"Who is that?" Cedric asked Bernard as he was led away.

Bernard glared at Scott over his shoulder. Scott huffed and stormed over to the woman right as Bernard pulled Cedric into the back room.

He pushed Cedric into a stack of frames leaning against the wall, and kissed him hard, probing his tongue deep into Cedric's mouth. Cedric's body lit on fire, and he gripped Bernard's strong arms, kissing him back hungrily. Bernard pulled away.

"Don't worry about that business." He pulled Cedric through the back door, out into the alley behind the building. "I brought you something."

Bernard reached into his black suit coat and pulled out a fat joint. He put it between his full lips and lit it up, taking a hit. "This has something special in it."

He took it in his long fingers and placed it in Cedric's mouth.

Cedric took a greedy pull, the cool, skunky smoke filled his lungs and soaked his brain. He closed his eyes, and he could see the Desmarais eclipse behind his lids, ablaze with its furious, cleansing sunlight.

He choked and handed the joint back to Bernard, running his fingers across the fine black fabric of Bernard's shirt. He looked so good tonight.

"Do you want to do it right here?" he asked.

Bernard's black eyes flicked up at him, flat, expressionless.

"Please, Cedric, I'm working." Bernard's tone severed the lovely smoky high, the buzz receding more quickly than it set in. Bernard was irritated with him. Annoyed. Patronizing. But why? Hadn't Bernard pulled him out here? And for what if not to fool around?

Cedric stepped back, and when Bernard held the joint out to him again, he shook his head. "No thanks."

Bernard's black eyes flashed. His face changed again, a sexy smile spreading across his lips. "C'mon, don't be gay," he teased.

"Fuck you," Cedric snapped. He was horrified by how hurt he was. He darted around the crumbling corner into the narrow alley back to the street. He needed to get away before the tears came.

"Baby, I'm sorry!" Bernard called. "I'm just tense about this exhibit."

Bernard was always like this, hot one minute, cold the next, but this time, something had changed. Cedric kicked through a pile of matting cardboard, wiping at his eyes as he stalked toward the street. He stopped next to a line of graffiti that said FUCK ARTS, still in the shadows of the alley beside the front of the gallery. He looked back and confirmed that Bernard had not followed him. Cedric hadn't thought he would. He took a few deep breaths and rubbed the rest of the sting from his eyes.

The gallery door opened. Scott stepped out, coaxing the homeless couture-wearing woman out with him. A sleek black town car rolled up to the curb in front of them.

Garret Green got out of the car and opened the door for a scrawny woman in a faded turquoise dress, with hair the color of dust and eyes so big and black Cedric thought he had underestimated his high. She lifted them up to where he stood in the shadows, and he froze under her gaze, her beautiful, horrible gaze. She was the artist of the paintings inside. He knew it without a doubt. Then she turned to Scott and the homeless woman, and her brow furrowed.

"Come on now, you need to get yourself cleaned up and take a nice long sleep, Dana," Scott muttered.

"I only wanted to see the exhibit." The woman sobbed, tripping over her bare feet. "I just wanted to see…"

She looked up into the black eyes of the artist and stopped in her tracks. She reached for her, but Scott tried to push her away.

"I just wanted to see," the woman whispered reaching out again for the approaching artist.

The artist took her hand, held it for a moment. Then let it slide from her grip as she walked past. Garret ushered her into the gallery, and the thunder of frantic applause followed.

Scott viciously shoved the dirty woman down onto her knees. Cedric was so shocked that he couldn't move. Nice Scott, his patron, his friend, was brutal with a woman who was obviously struggling.

"You dirty slut," Scott spat. "Get the fuck out, and don't come back. You're worthless now. You could open your veins and no one would care."

He kicked her, hard, in the ass, then spun on the heels of his patent leather shoes and stormed back into the gallery. The woman remained on her hands and knees, staring at the gum-crusted sidewalk. Cedric finally snapped out of his trance and went to her, squatting down beside her and taking her arm. She didn't move for a moment, her faded eyes fixed on the dirty sidewalk.

"Hey," Cedric said. "Are you okay?"

Her face snapped toward his, and she rolled back to her haunches. "They'll eat you up too," she whispered. "You should run now."

Cedric heard her but didn't process the words because he realized, now that he was close to her, that he knew who she was. Dana Glonciel. The best of the best. The cream of the crop.

And Scott Silver, who had been her patron too and, it was rumored, her boyfriend, had kicked her out of a gallery, shoved her over, called her a slut and told her to kill herself.

"Ms. Glonciel? Do you need help?"

"I need to get out of Dodge," Dana said.

Cedric felt something running through him. Something like fear. Something like hope. Something like the feeling the paintings inside the gallery had evoked. He helped Dana up and hailed a cab for the both of them.

Something was wrong. Something was different. Something was coming.

"She's spectacular." Mr. Black's smooth tenor voice almost purred, the way it did over his favorite artist and lovers. He was pleased as he sat down at the mahogany table.

"The talent oozing off of her is intoxicating." Mr. Silver drummed his fingers against the table top.

"Well done, Mr. Green. This one is your masterpiece."

"Truly well done," Mr. Silver echoed.

"Thank you, gentlemen." Mr. Green worked his fingernail into a groove beneath the table.

"We will throw a party for her," Mr. Black said.

"Yes, a big party. I will host it." Mr. Silver leaned back in his fat leather chair.

"I could host it," Mr. Black said. "Your parties have come to be expected. If I threw a party for her, it would create quite a buzz."

"My parties are an indication that an artist has arrived."

"But that is getting old, isn't it? Especially after everyone saw you with poor Dana." Mr. Black's voice dripped with false sympathy.

"No one even realized it was her, she was in such a state." Mr. Silver pounded the table with his fist. "And that was hardly my fault."

A piece of wood splintered off the groove under Mr. Green's fingernails.

"Are you suggesting it was mine?" Mr. Black asked. "I have my artists under control."

"Hardly!" Mr. Silver barked. "I heard Fleck stormed out of the gallery before Desmarais even arrived."

"He's fiery, but I always rein him back in. It's when he does his best work."

"Oh, so you are the good little muse, now?" Mr. Silver spat at Mr. Black.

"Enough," Mr. Green said. "The two of you have picked your favorites from the artists I've brought in over the years. I have never picked a favorite of my own. I am picking her, Terra. She's mine, and I will dole her out as I see fit."

Mr. Black and Mr. Silver both shook their heads in unison.

"Unacceptable," said Mr. Black. His smooth tenor pitched gravelly low and dangerous.

"Completely unacceptable," Mr. Silver echoed with a snarl.

"As soon as I find a new artist, one of you claims them and starts to feed."

"We groom them," said Mr. Black.

"We prime them to sustain us," said Mr. Silver.

"Well, I will take on that task with Ms. Desmarais," said Mr. Green. "I will get her ready, and I will make sure that she isn't destroyed before she produces her best work."

"She's a little gutter weed." Mr. Silver sneered. "She's already produced her best work."

"You'll exhaust yourself trying to get her in line," Mr. Black said.

"I don't care. Mr. Silver, I know you are feeling the loss of Glonciel, but it was your choice to cut her loose. And Mr. Black, I know Jackson is next, but he's got at least three exhibitions ahead of him and maybe more if you only would leave him alone."

"She's the best thing you've brought us in decades, Mr. Green," Mr. Black said. His handsome face twisted with lust and fury.

"You're trying to strong arm us," Mr. Silver barked.

Of the three men, Mr. Green was the one people noticed the least. The one they forgot the easiest. Mr. Green was not darkly handsome like Mr. Black, and lacked the wealthy flash of Mr. Silver. Mr. Green established himself best through a well-tailored suit and his earnest admiration for the art. After he introduced them to Mr. Black and Mr. Silver, his clients often forgot his name until they started on their downswing. Then it was too late.

Not this time.

"The girl doesn't feel comfortable here yet," Mr. Green said. "I will manage her, keep her out of trouble, get her what she needs and teach her how the city works."

"I can make her comfortable. I'll put her up in Park Avenue," Mr. Silver said.

"I'll make her feel so good, she'll forget her own name," Mr. Black hissed. "I'll dump Fleck for her."

"I've made up my mind on this," Mr. Green said. "Do you want to challenge me? Do you want me to start reeling in subpar talent?"

Denied their prize, the other two men glowered at him, but Mr. Green held himself stone still as he regarded them, his face stoic, his fingernail working into the widening crescent under the table. They needed him. They couldn't sniff out true talent like he could. He had Terra safe and under his care, for now.

Cedric didn't leave Dana's apartment for three days while she slept. He texted with some old friends, sketched in one of her blank pads, smoked a lot of pot and binge-watched her Netflix.

Cedric didn't have a TV, too much of a distraction, so it was like a vacation.

Dana Glonciel had good shit. A big-ass Greenwich apartment with a big ass TV with surround sound, a stocked wine cabinet, a loaded bar, and a master's degree from Tyler that qualified her to not only sell her world-famous art, but also to teach, lecture and write about it.

She also had a sister who kept calling and family pictures in the Hamptons. Dana came from money and made even more money.

And she was still a fucking mess.

He didn't leave. Not because of all her cool shit, but because he didn't feel like he could.

Dana thrashed in her sleep, muttering things like, "The mud is inside me," and "Please stop, I need that. It's all I have left."

Cedric tried to wake her up when the nightmares got bad, but she swung at him. Almost broke his jaw. He hoped what she really needed was sleep. After he had gotten her home from the gallery, and convinced her to shower, she'd been so exhausted, she practically passed out on her feet. He had tucked her into her bed and put a glass of water on her nightstand. Every morning he refilled the empty glass, so he figured she was okay.

There were messages from Bernard. Lots of messages.

Why did you run off?

I'm at your apartment. Where are you?

Baby, can we talk?

Cedric didn't answer them. He wasn't sure why. He thought he was in love with Bernard, but after seeing how Scott Silver treated Dana, something shifted.

He couldn't trust Bernard. He knew without a doubt that if he told him what he saw Scott do, Bernard would smooth him over and downplay the situation. He might even suggest Cedric hadn't seen it at all. That Dana was just seeking attention.

In the past, Cedric would have eaten that up.

Something was wrong.

On the third day, Dana woke up groaning as Cedric watched *Game of Thrones*. He brought her some won ton soup as she squirmed up out of her pile of blankets like a grumpy moth clawing out of a shitty cocoon.

"Who the hell are you?" she asked.

"Cedric Fleck," he said. "I brought you home a couple nights ago when you lost your fucking mind."

"I…" Dana's eyes darted across the floor, as if she was trying to find her mind there. Then she looked back up at Cedric.

"You're the pastel artist," she said.

"Yeah, that's me." Cedric couldn't help but grin. Crazy or not, Dana Glonciel was still a legend, and she knew who he was.

"What are you doing here?" she asked.

"Well, you kinda made a scene the other night, at the new exhibit down on Broad—"

"Terra Desmarais," Dana said. "Oh Fuck! Fuck fuck fuck fuck fuck! I didn't…Did I…? Cedric, I don't think I know where I've been all week. All I can remember are these fucking nightmares…"

Cedric handed her the soup. "For the past three days you have been here, sleeping."

"Sleep," Dana said. "All I needed was sleep, and he wouldn't let me. He kept…"

"Who?"

She turned toward Cedric as if she forgot he was there and shook her head. "So, what did I do?"

"You showed up at the opening kind of…out of it. No one recognized you though. Except Scott Silver. And he was…kinda a dick about it."

"What do you mean?" Dana asked, her eyes big and wary.

"I mean, when he thought no one was looking he…he hurt you."

Dana's jaw worked, clenching and unclenching. She started on the soup and slurped down the last of it a minute later. "Anything else to eat?"

"Girl, I will order anything you want."

"I want a pizza," Dana said. "A big fucking pizza."

12

"Another party?" Terra sighed. "I'm tired, Garret! I've been to parties every night since the opening."

She wore only an oversized t-shirt. One of Jim's maybe, and her pale shins were scuffed with blue bruises and flecked with paint. She had another masterpiece on her easel. A hint of a landscape, brown and black, with a brilliant blue sky, but a storm on the horizon. Mr. Green had to fight to keep his mind from wandering to the warm summer days of his twenties.

Terra was tired, and irritated with him, but he needed to convince her of this one last thing.

"It's a little one tonight. Only one critic, Bernard Black, the most important in the industry. And Scott Silver, a potential patron, will be there. He can set you up with a stipend to help you while you work."

"Why do I need that?" Terra cocked her head to the side and set her hand on her bony hip. "You don't want us here no more?"

"Actually, I love having you here," Garret said. It was the truth. On his free afternoons he would come into the apartment and find Terra painting something new. Something amazing. He would watch, and she was always okay with that.

His hair was growing in thicker. His grays were receding. The fine lines of his face filled in and his cheeks glowed with good health.

This is how it used to be, he realized. Strolling through the streets of Paris, watching the artists painting the Seine, stooping out of the hot sun under Roman arches to watch a cluster of students try to imitate Rembrandt. Feeling the vitality pouring off the canvases as each stroke pulled toward something closer to finished.

He'd always been able to recognize a masterpiece, and a master. Even before he partnered up with Mr. Black and Mr. Silver. It was, in fact, the best thing about him. And the most heartbreaking, for once they made their deal, Mr. Green wasn't just selling the art of his masters. He was selling the artists themselves.

Yet he needed not take anything to maintain his lifestyle. For so long he had been playing this game with his partners that he forgot the art itself sustained them. The artist channeled vitality through her, and all Mr. Green had to do to collect it was be in her presence as it spilled from her gifted hands. They had meant to be muses, elevating the talented up to heights they could never reach alone. That had been the intention. When had they gone wrong? When had they become so greedy?

"You are welcome to stay here as long as you like." Mr. Green cleared his throat, which had suddenly thickened with remorse. "I hope you do."

Terra chewed at her chapped lower lip and sniffed. "Well, I don't need much more. Like, this place is so swanky, and there's so much light to paint with. I just— I don't know why I gotta meet this Silver guy anyway."

"You really don't want more?"

Terra shrugged. "You said the paintings are selling real well."

"They are."

Terra's bony shoulders curled forward self-consciously. "So, I could maybe buy a rancher back home? With, like, an in-law suite for Jim?"

"Terra, honey, you could buy a villa back home, with a villa for Jim."

"I don't need nothing that swanky," she said, waving the idea away. "But I might wanna go home. You know, soon."

If she went home, that would be it. There would be no more sustenance. No more vitality. Silver and Black would destroy Green, and Green would be cut off.

This was why they got greedy.

Artists didn't make the best decisions for themselves. They gave up their careers for hot but useless love interests, for demanding, aging parents, for any number of bogus personal dramas. They spiraled out on drugs or sex or fame. They became reclusive weirdos. They joined political movements or cults and renounced their passion for saviors and gurus.

They decided to leave New York before their star had fully risen to move back to the sticks.

He'd insisted on managing Terra, so he had to manage her. Silver and Black had their ways of keeping their artists in line. Green had to figure out what his was. It was for the artists' protection as well as their own.

"Just this one last party, and then no more for a week. All right?" He smiled at her, and she smiled back, the corners of her lips fluttering as if she wasn't sure she trusted him.

Mr. Green wasn't so sure he trusted himself.

13

Dana Glonciel packed up to leave New York for good.

"I'm going to Myrtle Beach," she told Cedric. "My sister lives there, and I'm buying a house next to the ocean. I'm going to sleep whenever I want."

"What about your art?" Cedric asked.

"It's done," she said definitively.

Cedric hadn't thought there was any such thing as done for an artist. What had happened to Dana to drain all that drive out of her?

He helped her pack her car. Before she got in, she took his shoulder. "Hey, um, be careful, okay? This is a rough industry, and it's easy to let the bright lights blind you."

"Yeah, sure," he said.

Her fingers gripped the muscle of his arm, and she chewed her lower lip. "Before I had my breakdown, I, uh, I had some really crazy dreams. Nightmares. People I'd known forever turning into monsters. You—if you start to feel like something is wrong, don't ignore it, okay?"

Cedric nodded, her words prodding at the tightening knot in his diaphragm.

Dana handed him a slip of paper with a childish flower scribbled on it in pen. "My last work. It's for you."

And then she was gone.

Despite his unease, Cedric was not ready to give up his art, or his career. Dana Glonciel may have had a mental breakdown, but she also had millions in the bank and supportive family to nurse her back to health.

Cedric had debt, a studio he didn't own, and a show in a month. He had misgivings about Bernard, for sure, but he had to admit that Bernard took care of his career. And he needed his career. Bernard texted him, inviting him to a party for the new it girl, and Cedric accepted the invitation.

Something was wrong, sure. Rich people acting like dickheads wasn't anything new, though. Cedric just needed to keep his head down and his eyes on the prize.

He tried not to admit he was excited to see Bernard as well. The distance did not help him get over his toxic relationship.

Bernard embraced him at the door of Scott Silver's Park Avenue townhouse door, kissing his cheeks and then pulling back to look deep into Cedric's eyes. "I hope we are good again," he said. "I hate fighting with you."

The words rattled around Cedric's mind for a moment until they settled to the bottom, like coins rejected from a vending machine. Bernard loved to pick fights with him. Was he unaware or was he manipulative? Either way, Cedric had to admit Bernard looked hot tonight, too hot to be really mad.

"Cedric, old boy." Scott patted his back.

A hint of jowls jiggled at his jaw. Cedric had always envied Scott's effortless golden looks. It seemed like the man could just throw money at his reflection, and his reflection would pull itself together, but he looked puffy tonight, a pillow with a little too much stuffing. Or maybe that was the effort it took not to cringe when Scott touched him. Cedric couldn't forget him standing over Dana on the sidewalk.

Scott didn't seem to notice Cedric's discomfort. Maybe he didn't care. "Pleasure to have you join us.

We're still waiting for our guest of honor. She's quite the eccentric. Insists on bringing an old hillbilly with her everywhere she goes. The man is a riot, let me tell you."

"I've heard." Cedric kept his smile thin. He kept seeing Scott kicking Dana, telling her to kill herself.

"What have you been up to? Preparing for the May exhibit, I hope? Does your new studio get good light?"

Scott funded Cedric's studio. Funded his art. Funded his life.

Cedric had found success the last year, but it had taken a lot to get there, and he hadn't come close to reaching the kind of sales that would allow him to fund himself or give it all back to Scott. He let his smile spread to look more genuine. He had to walk the careful line.

"The new studio is great. And I'm excited about the series I'm working on. It's a—"

The door opened, and Scott unceremoniously spun away from Cedric and ran to the new guests with his arms open. So welcoming, so kind.

"You're late," Bernard said as Garret led the group of three into Scott's well-lit town-home.

"It's my fault, Mr. Black," Terra said. "I just lost myself in my work again. Takes Garret and Jim to drag me back to reality sometimes."

"Well, we certainly hate to disrupt a working artist," Scott said, clasping her bony hand in his fleshy one.

"It's all right," Terra said. "If I didn't stop sometimes, I would forget to eat."

Scott and Bernard laughed like it was high humor. Jim snorted. He was wearing a cheap blue button-down shirt with a stain on the belly and tattered jeans. Terra was in a faded green vintage mermaid dress that would have looked wretched on anyone else. On her, despite her awkward bones and jutting angles, it somehow looked like high fashion.

"Cedric, lovely to see you," Garret said, noticing him across the room. "Have you met Ms. Desmarais? I have not seen you at any events the last couple weeks."

Garret looked surprisingly well, in his bespoke gray suit, and Cedric found himself glad to see him. Glad he was there. Garret always offered straight advice. He always seemed to genuinely care about Cedric's career, and his well-being.

"I've been busy," Cedric said, feeling safe to approach the new star of the art world. He wanted to be jealous of her, wanted to hate her. She was already exceeding Cedric's sales, and she'd been out only a few months.

She smiled big at him, all crooked teeth and chapped lips, her odd dark eyes sparkling. She took his hand firmly into hers. He couldn't help but like her.

"Y'all do the pastel art, right? Damn, I love your work." She shook his hand enthusiastically, and he knew she was his people. Poor, earnest, with a burning, misunderstood soul that had been crushed from a young age.

"He is incredibly talented," Bernard purred, slipping his arm around Cedric's waist. Jim the redneck looked at that hand, and then up at Cedric. Cedric waited to see the disgust, the disdain, the hate he'd seen in the eyes of his teachers, uncles, priests when he was just a queer kid in Queens.

Jim's eyes held questions, not judgments. Then he looked away to take in Scott's grand home with the same discernment. His keen gray gaze landed on Scott. "You gonna offer us drinks or what?"

Scott's smile pursed. "Of course!" He released a stilted little laugh that was supposed to speak of Jim's rustic charm. He didn't fool anyone.

Scott disappeared into his kitchen and stalked out with with a tray of champagne flutes, which he held out with irritable flourish. Jim took a delicate flute with his sausage fingers. Scott handed one to Terra before she could take one herself.

There was a loud rap on the door.

"You're expecting someone else? I thought this was to be a quiet occasion," Garret said, his voice stretched like a rubber band wound around a toy, ready to snap and spin out.

"Just to round out the party." Scott's grin was rather wicked as he threw open the door to reveal the venomous smile of Kiki Michelle, with a gaunt but gorgeous companion. Kiki was a model, influencer and muse of the art world. Cedric had used her twice for an earlier collection until he found her sucking off Bernard in his bathroom.

Garret cringed at the sight of her. Bernard released Cedric's waist and Scott pulled her into his loft and spun her around in her flimsy gold mini dress, displaying her for everyone. She giggled, threw herself into his arms and pressed her thin lips to his for a deep and uncomfortable kiss. Her friend hovered in the doorway, scrolling through her phone.

Kiki turned to Bernard with a dramatic embrace, running her slender tan fingers down the muscles of his back and kissing both his cheeks. "I've missed you, baby," she said. Bernard had a sneer on his face as his eyes found Cedric's. It only grew as he looked back at Kiki.

A month ago, Cedric would have gone crazy with jealousy. He knew Bernard was bisexual, and hooked up with other people, but to flaunt it with a woman that he'd already…but tonight Cedric found himself too busy observing the dynamic. If Kiki was here then this was going to be one of *those* parties. He turned to see a mirror set on the polished lacquer table, a crystal bowl of tightly rolled joints, and another filled with a rainbow of stamped pills, all shining in candlelight.

He watched Terra Desmarais take several steps back to accommodate Kiki and her big gestures, her big purse, her big hair. Kiki's friend looked bored and plain, even in her expensive runway dress while Kiki soaked up all the energy from the room. Scott and Bernard smiled, their eyes weaving from face to face, sowing careful discord.

Garret gently took Terra's elbow, leaning in to whisper in her ear. Kiki wrapped her arms around her friend and dragged her into the room, speaking a mile a minute about her new line of handbags, and her recent trip to Paris.

"It was like I lived there in a past life." She laughed too hard, and Bernard and Scott laughed too. Cedric didn't think it was that funny and Kiki's friend gave a bored smile.

Scott and Bernard ate her up. Cedric held back, watching as Terra and Garret slipped away upstairs. He was tempted to join them, but more curious as to how Bernard would respond when he noticed they were gone. Jim had settled onto a couch playing with his mobile phone, drinking his second glass of champagne, completely unconcerned with what was going on.

That feeling Cedric had felt when he first peeled Dana off the sidewalk, coursed through him now. Bernard was an art critic. Scott a financier. Garret an art agent. They were friends, because they all worked in the same business. But there was something more.

Something wrong.

What was it that Dana had said to him, when he helped her up?

"They'll eat you up too. You should run now."

The toothy grins that Bernard, Kiki, and Scott gave each other were similar to the snarls of predators, circling a meal.

The parties with the partners used to be fun. Mr. Silver had a talent for dazzling the artists, and tearing down their inhibitions with top shelf entertainment. Now Mr. Green felt like it was the first stop on a conveyor belt that inevitably led to despair.

It was necessary.

To see where the artist's boundaries were. To see how pliable she would be. To see how she mixed when her defenses were down.

It was not ideal that Jim had tagged along. Both Mr. Black and Mr. Silver had raged against his inclusion, but Mr. Green had simply stated, "She will not come without him."

Inviting Kiki was a bold choice for Silver, one that could prove to be explosive considering her history with Black. Mr. Silver surely had his reasons. There was a way of doing things that Silver had maintained for all the years they'd worked together.

Kiki was a wild card, but she knew her part to play. With all eyes on her, Jim and Terra could get comfortable, and the party would really get started.

But Mr. Green couldn't get comfortable. He didn't like seeing Terra wilt beside the obnoxious, vampiric Kiki. Nor did he like the stricken expression on Fleck's face.

"Let me show you Scott's collection," Mr. Green said to Terra, while Kiki held his partners' attention in her perfectly manicured hand.

They slipped up the steps together, to Scott's private rooms.

When Silver had first bought the townhouse, fifty-two years ago, he had the upstairs gutted. All his living space was downstairs, on the first floor, and he circulated his pieces in the five spaces he deemed acceptable for art there, to make it appear that he was easily bored with the art he collected.

But the two upstairs floors told a different story. Silver kept work from every artist he'd ever sponsored up there in the climate-controlled space. The stone walls had become crowded so he ran heavy steel display racks between them, hung on both sides with Glonciels, Pollocks, O'Keeffes, Picassos, all illuminated with museum lighting, and kept in meticulous condition.

Scott Silver had a special talent for selling art at its peak.

None of the partners struggled for money. They all had property in New York, London, and Paris, where they split their years. But Silver had a nose for money like Green had for talent, and Black had for manipulation. Silver traded in real estate, junk bonds and art. He'd sold a DuChamp this year in a private auction for twenty-two million dollars. And he had five more.

Terra's breath caught in her throat as she cleared the second-floor landing.

"It's like a carnival!" she said.

The bright colors splashed all over the walls, the different styles and movements, all spinning around them like a festival. Being in the big, open room made Garret feel like a child, running down the dirt path to his grandpa's cottage, praying the old man was painting the sky again.

Garret had only one painting of his grandfather's, a small, stained canvas, he kept rolled up beneath his bed. He had not looked at it in years.

"Garret, how did Scott get all this work?" Terra stood in front of Silver's favorite van Gogh. It was easily the most expensive painting in the room and Terra, untrained as she was, moved her hands above it, like a blind person reading their favorite poem.

"He's worked with a lot of artists and private collectors over the years," Mr. Green said. It wasn't a lie. "Scott Silver can close any deal."

Mr. Green's ears popped, and he shivered. It felt like the temperature in the room dropped ten degrees.

Terra chewed at her chapped lower lip. "I don't think I want my art in here." She stepped away from the van Gogh and turned around, her expression strange. "It feels like a morgue."

Garret forced himself to laugh as his skin broke out in goosebumps. The gallery that had always awed him suddenly seemed garish. "What do you mean?"

"It's like he put them here to dissect them and see how they work. Let's go downstairs."

"There's another floor—"

"No thank you." She cut him off. Her black eyes caught the bright studio lights and flashed at him. He really could see no pupil within them. "It's my party, and they are all here for me. Let's go downstairs before they get upset with you."

Mr. Green watched her go, her normally slouched shoulders back, her scuffed thrift store heels clicking gracefully across the thick polished eighteenth-century wood planks. She was not herself. Her words, her mannerisms. The way she held herself was different. Had he turned her into an artist, so quickly? Or was he missing something?

He came down behind her in time to see Scott rushing toward her.

"I don't usually invite guests up to my private rooms." His smile was false, his pale brown eyes burning into Mr. Green. "But I hope you enjoyed it. Now, I am so sorry I didn't introduce you earlier, but this is my dearest friend, Kiki Michelle, and if you are ever in need of a human model, Kiki is the only option."

"Charmed!" Kiki stuck her hand out to Terra and curtseyed. Terra regarded her with slightly narrowed eyes.

"Kiki, have we met before?" Terra asked. Behind her, where he sat close to Kiki's model friend on the leather sofa, Jim cleared his throat loudly.

"Scott, we need some candy!" Kiki declared, ignoring Terra's reaction to her. "C'mon, Terra."

She wrapped her arm around Terra's skinny neck, and Mr. Green ran down the last couple steps to intercept.

Mr. Black grabbed Mr. Green's arm. "You seem so tense, Garret. Surely, you're not trying to kill our fun."

"Terra," Mr. Green said, pulling from Mr. Black's grasp. "You do not have to do anything you don't want to."

Terra turned her black eyes toward him as Kiki tapped the cocaine out of the silver compact, onto the mirror on the table and began to cut it into lines. There was a quirk of her crooked mouth, a tilt of her unplucked eyebrow.

"It's just a line, Garret," Terra said. "Loosen up."

Cedric felt déjà vu as the scene unfolded before him. Two years ago, this had been his party, with Cedric's hero, Malik Jackson, as a guest of Scott Silver. Bernard had brought Sheena Meegan as his date, and she had given Cedric his first big opening after the party. Garret had been by his side, telling him, you don't have to take that line, smoke that joint, suck that dick, but all Cedric had seen was Bernard's sexy gaze and the many zeros on Scott's check. Supplies he'd never dared to dream of affording, time and space and no more side jobs.

And the fucking drugs. They were top shelf. They still were.

As Cedric smoked a joint, wrapped in Bernard's arms, on the Italian leather sofa, he thought back to that first hit he'd done with Scott and Bernard and Garret. The beautiful explosion that set off in his brain, and the work it had produced for weeks, months to come.

Had it been the drugs? Or had it been the men?

Scott and Kiki made out on the couch across from him. Jim snorted a line with the model who no one had bothered to introduce. Terra began to spin around the room singing *Don Giovanni* in a ragged but perfectly pitched voice. Cedric felt reality squeezing in tight around him until it no longer felt real at all.

Something was wrong.

Bernard reached down his pants and Cedric forgot what it was. Before he succumbed completely, he saw Garret, good old faithful Garret, sitting in the corner, sipping from a small crystal glass of red wine, and frowning.

15

It all cashed in the same, time and time again. The hillbilly and the model were going at it in the guest room. Fleck was asleep on the couch. Desmarais sat at the black lacquered dining room table, swaying from side to side. Mr. Green could feel the waves of her essence rolling over him. The drugs, the sex, the company, it all acted like a catalyst to crack an artist open wide and let that magic within them truly flow. Everyone benefited from it, but the partners most of all.

"We can guarantee your success here," Mr. Black said, taking Terra's bony fingers into his hand, running his nails softly across the pads. "Success beyond your wildest dreams."

The artist chuckled and swung her arm away from him and around Kiki beside her, who was doing another line. Kiki kissed up Desmarais's arm until she reached her cheek and put her head against her shoulder. Terra laughed harder.

"What's funny, Terra?" Mr. Silver asked. The padding in his cheeks trembled slightly. Mr. Silver hated to feel like he was being made fun of.

"You sound like a couple of evil wizards, trying to get me to sell my soul." Terra giggled.

Mr. Green snorted.

Terra leaned forward and took the line Kiki cut for her. "That's enough," she said and Kiki nodded, obedient.

"I already have a penthouse set up for you," Mr. Silver said, cutting a line for himself.

"I want to do some art now," Terra said. "Will someone take me home?"

Mr. Black's laugh was like melted chocolate, smooth, sweet, and warm. "Beautiful girl, we will move heaven and earth for you."

"Just take me home." Terra yawned and ran her fingers through her mud-colored hair. She had never looked so good, never been so attractive.

Mr. Green looked from Mr. Silver to Mr. Black. They had all gotten a taste, squeezed only a little out of her tonight, but no one felt satisfied. Here she was the hottest thing in a house of hotness, and she was on her way out the door.

"Fine, yes," Silver said. "Go home if you want, but Terra—"

"Not right now." She stood abruptly. "Maybe next time. Garret?"

She wavered a bit, but Mr. Green caught her arm and helped her walk. At the doorway Terra turned.

"Kiki, are you coming?"

Kiki knocked back her chair jumping to her feet and ran to Desmarais. The partners had never seen Kiki run for anyone. She lounged, she fucked, she did enough drugs to kill an elephant. She did not run, not in a century.

Terra looked back at Silver and Black. "You know, they used to call me a witch." She winked at them as she, Garret and Kiki left the party.

When the door shut behind the three, Mr. Silver stood up, picked up the mirror on the table, still piled with cocaine, and smashed it on the floor.

"Don't lose it," Mr. Black said.

"Don't lose it?" Mr. Silver snarled. "Don't lose it? She was here, right in front of me! I could smell her bones! One real taste of her would last a thousand years, and yet Green takes her behind the curtain, ushers her out the door. He's sabotaging us, Black! He wants her all for himself!"

"He's cultivating her talent," Mr. Black said. "And keep your voice down."

He nodded toward Fleck, asleep on the couch, after a lot of high-grade marijuana and a very good blow job.

"Did you see how she turned Kiki around?" Silver hissed. "Kiki, Black. Kiki de Montparnasse!"

"If you cannot calm yourself, we will not continue this conversation, Silver," Mr. Black said. "I can see that Mr. Green is not good for the girl. Or maybe the girl is not good for him. We will have to try something new. I have been suggesting it for a while now but—"

"I don't give a shit about your suggestions!" Mr. Silver shouted. "I want it! I want her! She is everything I ever wanted! I want it all! If Green won't give her to me, I will take her myself and then I will—"

Black punched him in the face and Silver tumbled backwards over the table and onto the floor.

"Enough," Mr. Black barked. "We will discuss it in the morning, when you settle down."

"Fuck you, you Dada queer. You've been soft since Cocteau." Silver spat from the floor.

"And you've always been an entitled bougie piece of shit," said Mr. Black. "But we all have a purpose, and we're all in this together. Unless, you think we ought to wander back out to that French swamp to negotiate our contract?"

"Fuck you, Black," Mr. Silver grumbled.

"Fuck you back," Mr. Black replied.

On the Italian leather sofa, Cedric Fleck was not really asleep.

16

When Mr. Green arrived at the Soho flat, two days after the party, he was not sure what to expect. His partners had been very terse in their correspondence. Terra had not been answering the phone. Mr. Green was worried he had blown it all up, lost his master artist to appease his greedy partners, and perhaps himself a little as well.

Yet Terra answered the door with the same, fey, confused smile she usually had. There was no hint of the startlingly confident woman who had taken home Kiki, the hottest piece of ass for the last century. Terra had literally poached her from under Silver's nose and left the partners ravenous.

Mr. Green had alternated gloating and worrying for the last few days.

Terra itched at a mosquito bite on her arm, slouching, seemingly trying to shrink in the grand doorway.

"Terra, are you all right? I have been worrying about Scott's party ever since I brought you home. You said you didn't want to go, and I shouldn't have pushed you."

Terra hunched her shoulders into a kind of shrug. "It's okay. You know, I haven't never snorted that kinda blow. It was pretty nice."

"I—" Mr. Green stopped. Her confession threw him for a loop. Had he thought she was so innocent? So perfect? He stepped back, realizing he didn't even know how old she was. He thought Jim was some sort of father figure to her, but Jim was only in his mid to late fifties and Terra was…she had to be…

"How old are you, Terra?"

She hunch-shrugged. "Jim and I made pulled pork. You want some?"

"What?"

"Pulled pork? Jim makes his own barbecue sauce. It's real good."

She wandered back into the flat, past an oil pastel that made Mr. Green remember the first woman he'd loved. The one who made him think he would die when she married a rich merchant instead of him. The enticing smell wafting from the high-end kitchen was all that kept him from crying in the studio, and he turned to see Terra leaning against the door-frame, popping shreds of wet meat in her mouth.

"What is that?" he asked.

"You never had it?"

He went into the kitchen to see a slow cooker full of shredded meat in reddish sauce. It looked foul, but it smelled divine. Mr. Green had certainly heard of barbecue, and was not a fan, but pulled pork was not something he'd ever encountered. Terra slopped a pile of it onto a generic white hamburger bun and handed it to him on a paper plate.

Mr. Green had eaten Tarte Tatin on top of the Eiffel Tower, and Risotto al Tartufo Bianco in Saint Peter's Basilica. He took a tentative bite of the wet meat and groaned with delight. "This is heavenly."

"Told you," Terra said.

"Don't let him eat it all," Jim yelled from the bathroom.

Mr. Green took another big bite and spoke with his mouth full. "I came to ask if you would mind attending another gallery premiere."

Terra twisted her mouth up. "Are your partners going to be there?"

"Mr. Black and Mr. Silver are not my partners," Mr. Green said, a ripple of nausea sputtering through his belly. He set the pulled pork down on the polished rosewood kitchen table. "We are friends."

"Y'all don't seem to like each other much," Terra said. She slopped a wad of wet meat onto a bun and took a big bite. The juice ran down her chin and dripped onto the mahogany floor.

"They have helped the amazing artists that I've discovered succeed and thrive in the art community," Mr. Green said. "Artists like Malik Jackson. He was tagging walls in the South Bronx when I got him his first exhibit, but without Mr. Black, no one would have come, and without Mr. Silver, Jackson wouldn't have been able to keep producing such brilliant artwork."

"He would have stopped tagging walls?" Terra asked, her black eyes unnervingly locked onto Mr. Green's.

"No, probably not," Mr. Green said. "But he might have ended up in jail, or homeless. Now he has a big house in the trendiest part of Harlem."

"That Mr. Silver pays for?"

Mr. Green was beginning to feel very ill, and staggered back to the blue velvet sofa. When he'd bought the sofa, it had been considered junk, a useless relic of a bygone age. But he'd loved it, and kept it well cared for and now it made the studio-living room area a work of art. He cared about things, for more than what they offered him. He cared about Terra and Malik, and Cedric Fleck and Dana Glonciel. He wanted them to have success, money, prestige, but he also wanted them to have…

"Are you okay, Garret?" Terra asked, her voice flat.

Garret realized his head was pressed into the blue velvet and the room was spinning around him. When had he lain down? Why was his heart beating so strange? It fluttered, and thumped in ways he never recalled experiencing before.

"I'm not sure barbecue sits well with me," he said.

"I'll come to the exhibit," Terra said, as if all was well now. "I'd like to meet Malik Jackson. I know you are doing your best."

"I am," Mr. Green's head was light, and it felt like snakes were moving through his chest. It wasn't unpleasant anymore. It was almost familiar now. Hadn't he once dreamed of this same thing? The stench of marsh waters burned in his nose.

"Did he eat it all?" Jim lumbered out of the master suite, wearing a stained a-shirt. Something was different about him, but Garret couldn't focus. He was tired now and the snakes within him were moving toward his eyes.

"There's plenty for you," Terra said.

Jim took a fine china plate from the cabinet and slopped the meat onto it. It seemed to squirm, like baby birds seeking the worm.

"What's wrong with him?" he gestured to Mr. Green, who realized he was groaning softly.

"Barbecue doesn't sit well with him," Terra replied, no trace of concern in her voice.

For a second Mr. Green saw light flaring up behind both of them, brilliant, golden and hot. Then he passed out.

17

The black clouds rolled in from over the ocean, and the wind filled her up, an empty sail to be blown away. Tonight though, there was a substance to her, an anchor she didn't recognize. She drank her wine straight from the bottle and yelled at the storm as it drew closer to her.

The lightning hit the water, then the beach, and she leaned over the railing screaming, "Come on and get me already!" Relishing the way the electricity in the air charged through her sallow skin and buzzed in her weathered joints.

By the time Betts found her she was soaked to the bone, laughing at the charging darkness. Whatever was coming was here, and there would be no stopping it.

Dana slept that night, heavy with the weight of the wine, and she dreamed a slogging, wild dream of thick mud, and reckless boys. Bolstered by beauty and plenty of their own wine, they joined hands in the darkness.

They waded through the filth. They cut their wrists and made a promise and ate the secrets presented to them.

Bad boys made a pact.

And now the past was coming back.

18

Malik Jackson's work was marketed as "the gritty, ultra-realistic mood of the street," and if that wasn't the whitest thing Cedric had ever heard, he wasn't sure what was. But Jackson was a good guy. He had featured Cedric's work in his own displays when Cedric was first getting his feet.

Unlike Dana Glonciel, Malik Jackson and Cedric learned art the hard way. Without art, there was nothing between them and the abyss. If he hadn't discovered how slashing pastels across paper had driven off the darkness, Cedric would have ended up slashing a blade across his wrists. They never spoke about it, but Cedric could almost see the blood in Jackson's spray paint.

Bernard had asked Cedric to meet him there, but Jackson had asked him first. Cedric decided he was replying to the first invitation and not the second.

He walked along the faux walls made to look like slum alleys, hung with Malik's amazing, and some not so amazing pieces. It felt nothing like the streets. It felt nothing like the genuine emotion that Jackson's earlier work used to convey. Cedric kept walking to the back of the gallery, past Bernard, who was whispering to Sheena Meegan, who looked cute in a red dress. Bernard's fingers casually stroked the small of her back, playing her like a piano as she hung on his words. Past Scott glaring at a large piece like it offended him, although it already had his gold tag on it, claiming it.

Cedric walked through the office where Garret argued with the curator about Jackson's cut of the sales, and finally he pushed through the fire door into the real alley behind the gallery.

Malik Jackson slouched on a wood pallet, smoking a cigarette, his knees pulled to his chest.

"Hey man," Cedric sat beside him, mindful of splinters and snags in his suit pants.

"This is the end," Jackson said. "I'm done after this."

"No way," Cedric said. "That's a great exhibit in there."

"It's total trash, and don't condescend to me," Malik said. "There's maybe three good pieces in there. The rest are shit. People will buy them, because Bernard Black tells them to, but I know they're shit, like I know that I sold my soul for a nice house."

"Dude," Cedric said. "Come on in and celebrate. Take a few months off. I would kill to be where you are right now."

"You don't have to kill, Ced," Malik said. "Just keep grinding for the fame. It'll eat you up, like it did with Dana. You know she's living down in South Carolina right now? South Carolina!"

"She was in a bad place. She went down there to feel better."

"She was the best," Jackson said. "Then she lit up like paper and burnt into ash. That's gonna happen to me too."

"Dude, cut it out." Cedric nudged him. "You're worrying me."

"I have my mom, my wife and my two little boys, and all of them depend on me to make money doing this. What is this, Ced? It's smoke and mirrors. It's the whims of rich white people. And it's been eating me alive ever since I started making money doing it. Do you feel it, eating you?"

"Malik, baby, are you out here?" a woman called and Cedric turned to see her, perfect proportions in a tight white dress, hanging out the back door of the gallery. She was not Malik's wife, who was a petite woman with a sweet face. This curvy goddess barely seemed like a person, so much as sex on a stick. Even Cedric, painfully gay all his life, was turned on just looking at her. It made him feel a little sick.

When she spoke, Malik rolled his head back like her voice bewitched him.

"Yeah, I'm here." He stood up and brushed the dust from his meticulously tailored navy-blue pants.

"Bernard said to find you," she said, stepping out into the alley in impossibly high shoes, looking like the angel of art. Cedric desperately wanted to know her, to draw her, set upon a backdrop of yellow flowers. "That new artist is here. You gotta come meet her."

"Yeah. All right," Jackson said. He looked at Cedric but didn't seem to see him, as he stalked back into the gallery. Cedric took a cigarette from the pack he left behind and lit one up, smoking it to the butt.

Something was wrong.

Malik knew it, Dana knew it, and Cedric, no matter how he wanted to deny it, to keep striving toward the fame that was just within his reach, he knew it too.

"Cedric, are you coming in?" Bernard stuck his head out the door. "Terra Desmarais is asking for you."

Cedric crushed out the cigarette and got to his feet, moving toward Bernard's voice and realizing, as he did, that he had no room to judge Malik. He was Bernard's sometimes side piece. He ran when he was called.

Bernard took his hand and kissed his temples and fixed his hair and pushed him back into the faux hood gallery. Cedric staggered through the crowd until he saw Terra Desmarais next to a canvas Jackson had done with acrylic inks, featuring a gray street, a shadowy man on a flat wet landscape, his feet wrapped in roots. They sat on a couch next to each other, Jackson's girlfriend pressed against the wall nearby. Desmarais was holding Jackson's hand, tenderly. It reminded Cedric of the way she'd taken Dana's hand when she walked past her on her way to her first exhibit.

Photographers took pictures, people clustered around talking about the scene, which would make every art review tomorrow. Jackson's face was open, clear, almost blissful and Desmarais's was shadowed, even in the well-lit gallery. They were having a private conversation, under public scrutiny.

Something is wrong. Something is wrong. Something is wrong.

Cedric could feel it pulsing with his heartbeat. He could hear it in the curious murmur of the onlookers, and the indecipherable whisper of Terra Desmarais, speaking only for the ears of Malik Jackson.

Mr. Green's shoulders were bunched up to his jaw when he arrived at the brownstone for the emergency meeting. Mr. Black was already scowling at his seat in the conference room as Mr. Green slipped into his chair and found the groove beneath the table. He jumped at the sudden slam of the front door. A moment later Mr. Silver stormed into the conference room.

"Jackson quit!" he screamed, slamming his meaty fist down on the table. Mr. Green noticed, despite the many finishes the table had endured, that there was a fist shaped indent, on Mr. Silver's side.

"They all quit at some point," Mr. Black said, sounding bored. "But they all come back."

"He wouldn't even let me throw a farewell party for him," Mr. Silver cried. "And he paid me back all the money I had given him. Everything. He said he's moving his family to Delaware. *Delaware!*"

"What about his girlfriend?" Mr. Green asked. He hadn't heard a thing from Malik Jackson, which was odd because technically he was only Mr. Green's client.

Mr. Black's face puckered. "He broke up with her. And he told his wife about her. It's a setback. He has money but not that much. A year in a hell hole like Delaware, and he'll be back, begging us to take him in."

"He was almost tapped!" Silver raved. "That exhibit was his last, and then we would have fed!"

"We don't have to feed on every artist," Mr. Green said.

His associates turned toward him, really noticing him for the first time in a while. They saw his brighter, thickened hair . They saw the diminished lines on his face.

"You have been feeding on her!" Mr. Silver hissed.

"You cannot keep us from her any longer," Mr. Black said.

"I have not been feeding on her," Mr. Green denied. "I've only been—"

"Does her cunt taste like the mud you pulled her out of?" Silver asked. "That old taste of home, Green?"

"Where in the world is a frigid peasant such as yourself finding the kind of drugs to keep her away from us?" Black sneered.

"Enough!" Mr. Green sprang to his feet. His associates pressed back in their seats, startled by the uncharacteristic display of temper. Green was the quiet one, the weak one, the one easily led. He never asked for much. He took even less.

And he was indispensable.

"I don't know how I came to be so complicit to your greed," Mr. Green said. "We used to only take from the artists that were self-destructing. Do you remember that? Do you remember how we cried to take the last of Vincent's spark?"

"Times have changed," Black said, slicking his glossy hair back from his face. "They all spin out of control as soon as we set them loose. Are you saying we should waste all that untapped potential?"

"You either think me a fool or you are lying to yourself!" Green said. "You have destroyed every artist I've brought you for the last half a century! And so many of them—so many had bright futures."

"Calm down, Mr. Green. You act as though we murdered them," Mr. Black said. Mr. Silver was heaving, red faced on the other side of the room, but Mr. Black was calm. "We gave them everything they wanted. Fame. Money. Sex. Drugs. They wanted more and more and we gave willingly."

"Gave like the serpent of Eden!" Green said. "All the time draining them of their most precious asset, their talent, their spark! It was the same as murder, and you know it! So many committed suicide or OD'd."

"I have heard your darling Dana is doing quite well in South Carolina," Mr. Black said.

"No thanks to you!" Green's eyes were blurred with tears. "We started off pure! We loved the art and the artists. We wanted to bring their brilliance into the world. Do you not remember when we were young, in Venice? When you asked me to join you? Do you not remember our vow and the gift we were given, to inspire artists? To care for them? We were so happy then, and the world we made around us was so bright.

"We were given a gift in that swamp, and look what we've done with it!"

Seeing only memories through his tears, Mr. Green did not notice that Mr. Silver had risen from his seat.

"I remember a dirty beggar from Delft, pleading a novel appreciation of art due to his unknown grandfather's moderate provincial success," Mr. Black said. "You had a skill, and you served our needs, but no artist makes it without money and market. Hell, we raised total hacks to the roles of masters back in the nineteen hundreds when you last left to find yourself. They're still talked about today. You are a useful tool, Green. But any sentiment and good times you remember were only for your benefit. You remain a filthy pretender's grandson from Amsterdam. And as for that French swamp, I hardly remember it. I don't think it ever really happened. There is no God. No muses, no magic. It is business and pleasure, and we found the way to milk them both to our benefit."

Mr. Green spun toward Mr. Black, feeling those words lodge themselves into his chest. Had he truly been so blind to these men he called friends? Had he truly—

And that was where his thoughts dropped out, for Mr. Silver had come up behind him and hammered a brass Rodin into Mr. Green's skull.

20

Cedric Fleck knocked tentatively at the cobalt blue door of the Soho apartment, worrying his lower lip.

Something was wrong. Something was really wrong. The air stank with it. It shuddered through his limbs. Terra Desmarais's invite only made him more certain of it.

Jim answered the door, wearing a stained leather vest and pants, and glowered at Cedric. "Took you fucking long enough."

"I was in the middle of a piece," Cedric lied. The truth was he wasn't sure he wanted to come, to find out what was wrong after all the work he'd done to deny it.

"No, you weren't." Jim sauntered back into the apartment, leaving the door open for Cedric to let himself in. Jim looked different, even in the ridiculous outfit. Cedric realized that his exposed arms were not the pale flabby arms he expected of the middle-aged couch potato, but thick with bulky muscle. His stance was straight and tense.

"Why did you call me?" Cedric asked. He felt jittery. It wasn't any kind of drug thing, because he hadn't smoked or snorted anything for a week. Entering into the living room, he felt his heartbeat slowing in his chest. The room was draped in paintings, hanging on every wall, leaning up against every piece of furniture, flashing in the natural afternoon light. Cedric felt whatever it was the Desmarais work made him feel before, except stronger here. He felt young, sad, tired, energized. He wanted to lie on the paint-flecked mahogany floor and just breathe here for a while.

Terra Desmarais appeared in a bedroom doorway, looking like a wraith queen, pale skin stretched tight over angular bones, arms and Popsicle-stick legs jutting out of her faded black slip dress, her dull-colored hair piled on her head in a messy knot secured with, what looked like, a crown of twigs. Her black eyes regarded Cedric, and he finally realized what her paintings made him feel.

That twisting, awful, beautiful urge to create. That tender moment just before he put a piece of charcoal to a sheet, just before the dream began to take form when everything was possible. All of her pieces were all a hope of creation that Cedric felt so innately, he had not even recognized it was something separate than a constant state of life.

He opened his mouth, though he wasn't sure what to say. Terra put a narrow finger to his lips. "There isn't much time, so I want you to listen," she said. She was no longer the poor girl he had recognized as similar to himself. She was something else entirely now. "I have things to show you. You are a talented artist, and you have many years ahead of you. Your best work is yet to come, so listen."

Cedric felt a sensation like a corkscrew, twisting in his chest. Something was wrong, and he understood now that Terra Desmarais was at the center of it all, but was she the cause or the cure?

Jim settled on the blue velvet sofa and continued to glower. Terra moved the canvases leaning up against the glass top coffee table and indicated Cedric should sit beside Jim. Then she went into a bedroom and came out carrying a mirrored tray with a gold filigree rim, set with an old etched perfume bottle with a tasseled atomizer pump and a pitcher of water. She set them down on the coffee table and knelt before it, across from Cedric, removing the gold cap and diffuser from the perfume bottle.

"You have something very special, Mr. Fleck," she said, her black eyes locking onto his. "Something that is hard to recognize and impossible to reproduce."

She pulled a little blue bottle from what looked like thin air. Cedric couldn't look away as she removed its delicate stopper. A deep fragrance pervaded the room. It was the impossibly bright colors of the stained-glass windows of St. Patrick's Cathedral with the sun streaming through them, the deep-clean peace of copal incense after confession when Cedric was little, the first kiss with the first boy he loved, the enthusiastic praise from a woman observing his sketches of Central Park. It was all the unbelievable beauty that had twisted itself into his spirit and tried to bleed out in his pastels.

It was also the dark things. His father's backhand when he got distracted by the color of the sky, his mother's tears when she kicked him out onto the street after finding his hidden love letters, the enduring ever-burning fear of hell that bit at the heels of any happy relationship he attempted. The shame, the shame, the shame that the church he found most beautiful and peaceful rejected him for loving other men. The shame that he cut in black charcoal over his brilliant bright pastels.

"You understand, I think," Terra said, and Cedric realized he was crying. She didn't wait for him to answer, only for him to meet her unsettling black eyes again. Cedric was reminded of Bernard's eyes, so black he couldn't see the pupil, but Bernard's eyes were flat, guarded, blank. Terra's were blacker, darker, like staring into the void between stars and knowing there were galaxies there.

Terra dipped the glass stopper and dripped several pale blue drops of the powerful fragrance into the perfume bottle. "It's precious," she said. "A little bit goes so far."

She set the bottle aside and picked up the pitcher of water. "And this is what you need, to feed it, to sustain it, to live. It's vital, but you have to know when to stop."

She poured it slowly into the perfume bottle, and the oil on the top lifted higher and higher.

When the water filled the bottle, the oil spilled out over the edge. Terra, wiped it away and the fragrance faded. She put the gold cap back on and squeezed the ornate bulb, spraying the atomized water at him. He wiped the odorless mist from his face.

"This is pretty, but it's worthless," Terra said. "Everything special about it was pushed out trying to fill it up with more than it needed. Do you understand? That precious core must be preserved."

Cedric found he was still sniffing in long breaths, trying to catch that scent again. He thought he understood what she was saying, but why was she being so vague and weird? Beside him, Jim continued to glare at the table, like a gargoyle, a dangerous guard of times past. Terra picked up the perfume bottle and carried it into the kitchen. Cedric was tempted to filch the bottle of precious oil and run, but, as if he knew his thoughts, Jim turned his glare toward Cedric. Cedric tucked his hands between his knees.

A moment later Terra emerged from the kitchen with a bottle of vodka in one hand and the empty perfume bottle in the other. Cedric leaned forward on the sofa, riveted by the strangely fluid motion of her angular body. She knelt before the table again.

"What you need," she said, dropping three more aquamarine-colored drops into the bottle, "is to diffuse the gift with a strong base."

She tipped the vodka over the perfume, pouring about a tablespoon directly into the narrow mouth of the bottle. Not a drop spilled, and the oil began to bleed into the vodka, losing none of its color, although the scent in the room dulled and Cedric's tears dried on his cheeks.

Terra then poured a little water in, "Then you take what you need, and even if you spill over, it is not all lost. But you need a strong core. You need to nurture the gift, and sustain it."

She capped the perfume bottle and shook it vigorously and then handed it to Cedric. He took it reverently, gazing at the aquamarine essence inside.

"Spray it now," Terra said, and suddenly Cedric was afraid to waste even a drop of it, but although her voice was soft, he did not think her words were a request. He sprayed it onto his throat and rolled his head back, letting the fragrance run through him. The smell of his childhood apartment just before rain, the smell of roses in his sister's garden, the smell of summer days running through the streets and alleys with his friends, pastel dust, pencil lead, his first boyfriend's breath on his neck, the first twenty-dollar bill he'd been paid for an art piece, the blood on his lip after he stood up to his father…

"You understand." Terra smiled, and her smile was more brilliant than every cathedral and every perfect summer day. Cedric saw the galaxies in her black, black eyes and how short his time was, and how much shorter it would be if he did not care for that precious essence within him.

"I understand," he whispered.

"You keep that. It's for you, in case you forget. Now you must go hide in the master bathroom. Sit in the soaking tub and continue to listen."

"Listen for what?" Cedric asked.

"I am sorry, Mr. Fleck," Terra said. "Things are moving now, and I cannot stop them. I never wanted this. I was very happy painting in my modular with Jim next door. We had a good arrangement, but now my hand has been forced. Wayward children must have their toys taken away, when they insist on testing boundaries. I try to be a good mother."

Cedric thought that she was insane, and that she was the most beautiful creature he'd ever seen. He wanted to run, but he wanted more to obey her. He went through the master bedroom into the master bath and lay down in the extra-large soaking tub, clutching the precious perfume bottle to his chest and breathing in the scent on his shirt.

From the living room, he heard a knock on the door.

"What the fuck do you want?" Jim grumbled to the caller.

"Ms. Desmarais?" a voice Cedric recognized as Bernard's called into the apartment. He almost climbed out of the tub to go see him. It had been a week since he'd last laid eyes on Bernard's beautiful face, and it had been ages since they'd made love.

A waft of the strange perfume stopped him. "Listen," Terra had told him.

"Ms. Desmarais," Bernard called. "We are dreadfully sorry to stop by unannounced but you must get ready right away. The most important people in the art world have gathered at Mr. Silver's house, and they all are dying to meet you."

"Get the fuck out of here," Jim said. *"Game of Thrones* is on tonight."

Someone else laughed sharply, and Cedric thought it sounded like Scott. What the hell were Scott and Bernard doing at Terra's apartment? What party? Why wasn't he invited?

"That is quite a get-up, Jim," the other man said. It definitely sounded like Scott. "Do you dress in character for the show? I never realized you worked out."

There was the tap of fine shoes across the hardwood as the men let themselves into the apartment and came into the living room.

"Oh my, she has been busy," Bernard murmured.

Scott sniffed the air. "Mr. Black, I have never been so hungry."

"A feast indeed," Bernard replied.

"What are y'all doing here?" came Terra's voice from the room across the hall from Cedric.

"Ms. Desmarais, I am sure you are quite busy, but your entire career hinges on this party," Bernard said. "Brilliant and important people will be there for you. You must get ready right away. I brought you a dress. It's a Dosecure."

Scott said, "It'll be a night that people will speak of for years to come."

"Where's Garret?" Terra asked. "I haven't heard from him all week."

"Garret will be there as well," Bernard said. His voice was so smooth and seductive that Cedric was surprised by the certainty that he was lying. Had he always been able to tell that Bernard was full of shit?

"Then why hasn't he called me?" Terra asked. "I don't like to do nothing if he doesn't tell me to. I'm sorry, guys. *Game of Thrones* is on tonight. Jim and I watch every week. I can meet your swanky people tomorrow."

"I don't think you understand, dear," Scott said, his voice dipping.

"You are the guest of honor," Bernard cooed.

"You really must come."

"We insist."

"If you don't, your career will be ruined."

"No more nice apartment."

"No more drugs."

"No more money."

"No more girls."

"Oh well," Terra said.

Cedric almost snorted. The both of them were such bullshitters, and she didn't even care. But the worst part is that he'd heard this speech, from both of them, at least twice before when he'd wanted to take a break and dry out a bit. And he'd fallen for it both times.

"Well, it's hardly convenient to do it here, but fine," Bernard said, his voice taking a turn into something sharp and dangerous. "Garret tried to keep you for himself, and that is unacceptable. Come with us to a party, Terra, and we'll all have a good time."

"Hey!" Terra yelped.

"Let go of her, you fuckers!" Jim thundered.

"Oh, no need for profanity, old boy," Scott said. There was a metallic click, a gun being cocked. "Do you like my piece? It's vintage. I don't only collect art, you know. But I assure you, it works perfectly well at putting holes in bodies."

What was happening? Bernard and Scott were kidnapping Terra at gunpoint? What the hell was going on?

"You gave them every fucking chance," Jim snapped at Terra.

Terra sighed heavily. "I guess so."

Then there was screaming. So much screaming.

Mr. Green awoke at the long mahogany conference table. The stench of blood was thick in his nose. His skin itched, furiously. He was bound to his plush seat with stinging nettles. Confused, he squirmed against them, and they tightened, their barbs biting through his filthy shirt into his skin. He stopped that business immediately and looked about the room.

He'd been locked in the basement that they reserved for their runaway artists, with no food or water. He had lost track of time, so he was unsure how long his associates had been making trouble in his absence, but from the looks of things it was very, very bad.

The candles in the crystal chandelier emitted a strange, red flickering light, making it challenging to see what was real in the long conference room. Shadows seemed to move in and out of the paneled walls. A low, deep hum resonated through the air, aching in Mr. Green's eardrums.

Mr. Black and Mr. Silver were also bound in their chairs at the table. Mr. Black's handsome face was crusted with blood, and he had a nasty gash at his temple. His shirt was torn open, and there was some sort of black filth caked on his lean chest. His head lolled to the side, and his eyelids flickered.

Silver's cheek was torn open, dripping a thick slime of clots through trembling yellow globs of fat. The nettles were wrapped tight around his chest and arms, blood blooming through the fabric beneath them. His gray eyes opened on Green's, and he began to thrash against his bindings as if he could break them through pure fury. They only tightened more and more, squeezing into his bulging flesh.

Silver screamed, awakening Black. Black struggled for only a moment before he caught onto the tightening bindings; his eyes rolled frantically around the room.

"What did you do?" Mr. Green demanded.

Black barely acknowledged him. He took a deep breath and thrust against the nettles in an attempt to break through. Instead, they cut into his clothes.

There was a tugging at Mr. Green's feet, and he saw black roots writhing up from the floor, climbing his pant leg. The wet roots coiled around Black and Silver's necks. Silver finally stopped struggling, his eyes wide with panic.

"What did you do?" Green shouted at them. He had his own head wound, a throbbing knot where Silver had cracked his skull. He wouldn't have survived it if he was a normal man. He wasn't sure that Mr. Silver knew that it wouldn't kill him. He wasn't sure it mattered if he did.

These men were not his friends. They never had been. Mr. Green had spent several lifetimes deluding himself.

"I don't fucking know!" Mr. Silver cried, frenzied as the roots worked their way up his face, hair-like tendrils probing his open cheek. "Do you think we did this?"

Mr. Black groaned. The roots wove through his hair, creeping down his shoulders, spreading over him like ink on wet paper. "The girl." He panted, trying to gain control of himself. "That bitch and the old redneck—"

His words were clipped off by the rattle of the paneled door as Jim lumbered into the room, a forge hammer slung over his shoulder. It would have been comically large if it didn't look so menacing in his massive hand. Mr. Green recalled he had been a welder. He had a bad back. He lived in a trailer park, for God's sake, so why did he look like he'd been born with a fifty-pound forge hammer? Why did he look like he stepped out of Greek myth, with massive pythons for arms, and his polished bronze breastplate?

"What the fuck?" Mr. Silver screamed, accurately summing up all of Mr. Green's questions.

Jim leaned up against the wall and grinned at them, showing a mouth full of bright teeth, sparkling in the red light.

The roots at Mr. Green's legs crept up to his waist. Mr. Silver started to scream as the ones around his face worked their way under his skin at his cheek. Mr. Black, too, hissed as wet black tendrils grew into the gash on his head.

Silver bucked against the nettles, bleeding through his torn suit, fighting as hard as he could to get his arms free.

Jim chuckled, like their torment was a fun joke. The breastplate was the sort of craftsmanship that would make a museum curator drool. Jim's greasy fringe of hair had been buzzed smooth, and he looked like an ancient Greek general.

"Fuck," Mr. Black uttered, remaining still as the plants continued their path over his hands. The deep resonance turned into a rumble in the earth. Across the table from Mr. Green, where no one had ever sat, jagged spires broke through the Italian marble floor. Spikes of polished bronze rose higher and higher until the gleaming ebony seat, gilded with platinum filigree, was revealed. A throne, woven in weeds and gold, a soft cushion of raw silk awaiting a regal ass. The rumbling stopped, the throne fully ascended, and Jim opened the door. A procession of four beautiful women in brown silk chitons walked in, each carrying a different item.

Kiki de Montparnasse, darling of dada, led the procession, holding a gold tray of crystal. An antique Baccarat decanter and four matching flutes. She set it on the table before the throne and the gorgeous, green-eyed woman behind her set a glass in front of each of the partners. The third woman brought flowers, water lilies and irises, which she draped all over the beautiful and terrifying throne, and the woman behind her entered playing a lute, plucking melodies that pinched something deep in Mr. Green's heart.

Tears streamed down his cheeks. Even his partners had wet tracks through the blood on their faces. Mr. Green felt as if he teetered on the edge of an abyss, exhilarated by the rush of potential flight and crushed with the dread of the fall. His tears turned to silent sobs, his chest heaving against the nettle barbs in his skin.

Terra Desmarais entered the room with a rush of hot air. She was not Terra Desmarais anymore.

She wore a gown as black as the abyss, but somehow sparkling like a star in the wilderness sky. On her head she wore a crown of twigs, studded in rubies. She glided over the path of flowers, her irises expanding to fill her eyes with blackness. Her women took their places behind all of the seats at the table.

Terra stepped up to the throne and regarded them all with her endless eyes for a moment before lowering herself to her seat with feral grace. Mr. Green had never seen her move like that. He felt as if he'd never seen her at all before now. Kiki filled Terra's glass from the decanter, then passed it to the woman next to her. She filled Mr. Black's glass and passed it to the woman standing behind Mr. Green. It went around the table until the decanter was empty and each of them had a crystal flute of pale blue liquid on the table before them.

"Terra," Mr. Silver's hoarse voice teetered on hysteria. "Whatever you think you're doing—"

"No," Terra said softly, raising her hand. Scott shut his mouth. "This is my party. You insisted I come. Now we will drink to me."

The binding plants fell away from their wrists. Mr. Green cried out with pain and relief, rubbing feeling back into his aching hands. The woman behind Mr. Green had long brown braids and skin that glowed in the candlelight. She met his eyes as she picked up his glass and handed it to him, and his tears began again. He had seen her before, but he couldn't say where. In another life, another place. Italy during World War II? Morocco in the Jazz Age? London during Victoria's coronation? All the memories flooded through him, overwhelming him.

"Thank you." Mr. Black's smooth voice broke Green from his overpowering melancholy. His partner was practically purring as he accepted the glass from the green-eyed lady, who also looked familiar. Black had gained enough sense to try his hand at seducing his way out of this.

The sound of shattering glass broke Black's fragile spell.

"Get away from me, you cunt!" Mr. Silver had smacked the crystal out of the hand of the woman giving it to him. He swung for her again, but she stepped out of his reach, so instead he tore the roots out of his face, long bloody strands clumped with bits of gristle as they came.

"I won't drink your poison," he spat at Terra. "You dirty little gutter whore. I don't care what sort of tricks you are playing. This will end with my hands wrapped around your throat!"

"Mr. Silver!" Mr. Black hissed. "Show some restraint!"

"Shut up, you fucking pretender!" Mr. Silver screamed, spit spraying. The roots pulling from his face were continuous, and he yanked hard, tearing his cheek open wider.

"Silvio Medici." Terra's quiet voice resonated through the room. Mr. Silver's stopped pulling, stopped shouting. His eyes widened, and his mouth quivered. Terra smiled; her blackened lips curled with wrath. "You have always been a man who demanded the best. Silver was a fitting name to take, coming from a family of limitless wealth. And yet you were cut off from that wealth."

"Shut up," Mr. Silver croaked, the bulge of his throat bobbing, blood spilling from his mouth.

The threads finally started to connect in Mr. Green's mind. Dana's recovery from total despair.

Jackson's sudden departure. The afternoons watching Terra work and the sudden vitality in his appearance.

The stench of decay, mud and stagnant water, the marshes overpowered the coppery smell of blood.

It had been so long ago that they had made their vow, their pact, and even then, it had been half a joke. A drunken farce into the black marshes in some forgotten French village to call upon a local legend, a bog witch, a fairy, a goddess who granted favors.

They had seen nothing. Heard nothing. Drunk and young, and steeped in a friendship that seemed deep and real, they had eaten the black roots and made promises to the night. When they got tired, they stumbled back to Scott's—Silvio's—chateau, leaving thick mud prints in their wake that the maid had wept over.

They hadn't even considered that it worked until they realized that their friends and artists were aging and dying.

And they were not.

There had been nothing since then, except the never-ending stream of abundance. More and more and more and more until they forgot how they came to be so lucky and simply sought the next thrill.

"Toast with me, Silvio." Terra lifted her hand, and from the floor Mr. Silver's shattered glass pieced itself back together, complete with the pale blue drink inside and landed in his hand. Terra stood. "All of you, toast with me. For I am the artist of the hour. My work has made you all millions in the few short months I have been your pet, and yet you are so hungry you would eat me before I even reach a year. Toast with me, for I am where the line was crossed."

Mr. Silver struggled to throw the glass again and screamed. Slender vines burst out of the skin between his fingers, twisting around his hands and raising the glass to his lips. He pressed his mouth shut but the black roots broke out through his other cheek, curved through his pressed lips and pried them open. They filled his mouth, wrapping around his molars as the vines tilted the drink in. Mr. Silver started to spit it out, and choked. The roots sealing his mouth shut and filling his nostrils. Terra smiled serenely as Mr. Silver finally was forced to swallow.

Mr. Black drank his own drink quickly, grinning at Terra as if to prove he was a willing captive. Mr. Green looked into Terra Desmarais's eyes and raised the glass to his lips and drank. If he was to die tonight, he would die penitent. It was a fresh, sweet wine that went down easily. Mr. Green resigned himself.

Terra Desmarais drank hers too and then laughed, and threw her glass down, smashing it on the ground.

"It is fun! Isn't this a fun party! But I am missing *Game of Thrones*. Kiki, what channel is *Game of Thrones* on?"

Terra waved her arm and the panel hiding the large LCD screen TV rolled open and turned onto *Game of Thrones*. At the door, Jim cursed.

"We missed the beginning," he grumbled.

"Maybe we can rewind." Terra handed Kiki a remote. Then she turned back to the men at the table.

"And so, we are here. Silvio Medici, Bertram Hassan, and Gareth Vermeer." She smiled wide, and her teeth were sharp. Her black irises bled out until both her eyes were voids. So were the eyes of Jim and the ladies serving her. "I appreciate the new names. A bit on the nose, but I don't mind. Silver for your money, Black for the newspaper ink, and Green for the new talent you bring in, Gareth. Perhaps we should drop pretense, though? I used the name Terra, but I am Goddess. You called upon me more than three hundred years ago, and I granted you my gifts, to inspire and bring forth my artists. To shelter and protect them, to cultivate them and spread their beauty into a desperately wanting world. Do you recall that?"

Mr. Green slumped against the nettle bindings, no longer feeling their barbs. Something moved in his chest. It was finished. What he had set upon with such earnest hope had been corrupted by his own greed. Now it was time to pay for what he had taken. His fingers worked beneath the table until he found the splintered groove he'd been working at for the last twenty years.

"Fuck you, witch!" Mr. Silver's hands were again bound to the chair but he spat roots from his mouth. "You're nothing. You're garbage."

"Silvio." Goddess clucked her tongue with disappointment. "Your want for pretty things…" She wagged her finger. "You never learned how to hear no. When you raped your lovely cousin and your family cast you out, you stole as much as you could from your father's home and started acquiring new pretty things. Whether you had to buy them or steal them. You did inherit your family's talent for money, but that is all you inherited, isn't it? When I accepted you, I knew you would invest in my babies and make more money. I didn't think you would be so bold as to steal from them too. I saw your collection. I know what you did."

"Bitch!" Blood sprayed from Mr. Silver's furious mouth. "I earned everything I have! I have worked every day of my life to—"

"Shut up now," Goddess said.

Mr. Silver's sudden screams were muffled as black tendrils burst through his jaw and tangled, twisting in, over and through his lips. Mr. Green's skin itched, and he saw with numb terror that the veins on his hands bulged with the same roots, moving beneath his flesh. He thought perhaps they had always been there and only now burrowed through their bodies, activated by the presence of their mother.

"Are you saying we failed, somehow?" Mr. Black interjected, his voice incredulous, the desperation beneath barely noticeable as the roots climbed beneath the smooth flesh of his cheek. "We have brought more great artists into the light than anyone before us. We have faithfully brought you the most glorious talent in the world, and we have fostered them to heights that none of us could have imagined possible when we first started. Our talent is known on every page of art history. It is iconic! It is perfect! How have we failed you?"

The goddess turned to him and smiled. "Ah, Bertram the seducer, fucking your way up then looking down at all those you left in your wake. Yes, you have a talent of the tongue, but do you really think you can seduce me?"

"I am merely asking, Goddess. Have we not done all you asked and more? We have done this for centuries." Mr. Black managed to pull together a decent smoldering look even with crusted blood and creeping plant matter on his face. "And every year we bring more and more artists to the spotlight, more than ever before in history. But it does take a toll on us. When they start to fade, when they cannot produce anymore, all we do is take a little bit to help us carry on."

Goddess smiled with her sharp teeth but not her black eyes. "Take a little bit?"

"Do you not receive power from those who excel in your name?" Mr. Black asked. "Is that not why you imbued us with our talents?"

"No! Wrong!" Goddess shrieked and the roots burst through their eardrums and wrapped around their throats. Mr. Green wept with the pain as blood and wet foliage ran down his face. Terra's crown of twigs writhed on her head as she turned her attention toward the TV. Her mud-color hair dripped down her back, splattering all over the floor and her dress swirled like whirlpools, into oblivion.

"Arya is my favorite," Jim said.

Then the roots were in their eyes and everything was black.

Mr. Green was on the black lacquered dining room table of Mr. Silver's Park Avenue town home, but his body was wrong. It was frail, narrow, and so incredibly tired. A great emptiness seemed to spread, cold and creeping inside his aching chest. Everything hurt. He just wanted sleep. If he could sleep, he might feel better. He might be able to think.

The singing kept sleep away though. It was too beautiful, too powerful to resist, like angels, the secrets of the universe right behind the melodies, waiting for him to reach out and crack them wide open.

"Just breathe, Dana," a voice said in his ear. His voice. He opened his eyes to see his own eyes, wet, and full of pity, looking down at him. Then he, the he outside of himself, placed his lips against the bare belly of the him on the table, and sucked.

He had never seen it before, the pores that opened up in his skin, hundreds of hungry little mouths with black root tongues, wiggling perversely, chirping like angelic crickets, as he kissed the goose-fleshed skin of his artists.

It hurt, oh hell it hurt, but not a pain he'd ever felt before. They were emptying him. Scott, snorting cocaine off his fish-belly-colored thigh pulled life right out of this body, into the chomping cavities in his hateful face, while others opened in his throat, calling that searing siren song. Garret had never heard it before like this, sickening, seductive.

And then Bernard placed a cold hand on his forehead.

"You're always a good time, Dana." He spoke out of both sides of his face, a jagged-toothed mouth on either cheek as the one in the center licked its lips before kissing him. Bernard's hot tongue probing his throat, scraping the little bit of life left out from inside him.

He tried to fight. He tried to scream but the body leaned into it, still enraptured by the song, still thinking that this was the only way forward.

"You're killing me!" he tried to scream, if to no one else then to himself.

He knew where he was, who he was. He knew he would not listen. All his fine intentions and lofty ideals, but he still recalled the taste of Dana Glonciel on his lips. Nectar and sunshine, the bright gold burn of perfect creation, coursing through his veins as he sucked her dry.

Now he was on the other end, and the cold void within him became a vacuum, sucking away all the light and color from his life. He hated the man at his thighs, the man in his mouth. Most of all he hated the man at his belly, who dared to glance up to meet his eyes and shed a pathetic fucking tear.

How dare he cry for Dana while he fed on her! How dare he pretend to fight for Malik Jackson or Cedric Fleck. He fucking knew they all ended up here sooner or later. His weak words never stopped that descent.

"Almost done, Dana," he said to himself, the hungry mouths all smiling back at him, licking crumbs of life off their lips.

Mr. Green sobbed as the roots pulled back from his eyes. Mr. Silver's eyes rolled back into his head, and he wavered against his bindings.

"How were we to know?" Mr. Black cried out.

The goddess raised her hand, and the roots growing from his face and ears filled Black's mouth. His handsome face turned red, then purple as he gagged against them.

Goddess turned her terrible black eyes to Mr. Green. Her own skin squirmed with roots and nettles. They had called to her as young men, centuries ago. They had eaten the swamp plants that only grew in that marsh. They had taken her into them, and she had given them part of herself to spread her gift. Now she would destroy them for abusing it. "You have not yet made your argument," she said.

"I have none," Mr. Green said. "What I have done has been despicable."

"Humility only takes you so far, Gareth," she said. A lopsided smile rose on her lips, and he saw a trace of the Terra he had known. The goddess pulled a brown sprout from her black eye and examined it. "Does it surprise you to learn that your associates are both pretenders? That they were not who they said they were when they took you in? I assure you, neither of them knew the other was false when they teamed up.

Even now, they are angry at each other for their facades, when they have spent their whole lives judging others for such things. Do you remember how they treated my poor Vincent?"

"He was a brilliant man, but a troubled man," Mr. Green said. "Perhaps he had too much of your gift."

"Perhaps." She flicked the sprout away and turned back toward Mr. Green, baring her sharp white teeth. "But he was not yours to take."

"I will not defend it," Mr. Green said as the roots clutched to his skin, working their way into his pores.

"You're a fool, Gareth Vermeer! Weak and easily led."

"I resign myself to your judgment."

She smiled and turned toward the TV. *Game of Thrones* was still on, and Jim and the ladies cheered at some action on the show.

"The trial is well overdue," she said, the TV flickering in her dark mirror eyes. "I avoided it last time I was here, because there is always so much to see in a lifetime. So much to do. Last time a war had just ended, and there was vaudeville and dada and Kiki. Kiki remembered the pact she made, though. Unlike you three."

"I did not forget, Goddess," Mr. Green said. "I held it true to my heart all these years, but I—I—"

"You have a weakness of character." Her voice softened, a mother gently chiding a child.

"I didn't think—"

She slammed her fist on the long mahogany conference table. "You have a weakness of character!" she demanded. The old heavy table top flipped over like it was a sheet of paper, revealing its underside. It was pocked with the notches Mr. Green had worked into it over the centuries.

"Every time you disagreed with your partners," she hissed. "That is where you buried your objections. You are a coward, Mr. Green. Not a liar, or a seducer, or a thief. But a coward."

The notches were all around the table. Every time they had moved, changed identities, they had changed their places at the table, but the table had remained the same long mahogany table that Scott Silver had kept when they all first teamed up. And Mr. Green's fingernail worries dented the entire bottom. Every time he'd been overruled. Every time he'd bitten his tongue.

He looked to his partners. Mr. Black had passed out, asphyxiated by the coiling tendrils. Mr. Silver's mouth was sewn shut by the goddess's black threads, but his pale eyes glared at Green, dripping with contempt.

Had Mr. Green ever truly thought they'd known better than him? That they had power over him? Or had he been too afraid of their judgment, their disdain, to fight?

"I am a coward," he finally admitted, hanging his head, waiting for the roots to consume him.

"But you stood up for me," she said, again taking on a motherly tone.

Mr. Green sobbed. "Did I have a choice?"

"Silvio and Bertram sensed my power and went mad with greed. You sensed it, and you shielded me from them."

"Barely."

"Indeed." She stood up. "I have rendered my judgment. Kiki, pause the show."

Kiki did as she was ordered, and Jim and the women all gathered behind the goddess.

The goddess raised her hands, and the roots fell from the bodies of her captives, in a wet splatter on the ivory floor. Mr. Black awoke, gasping and choking, clawing at the phantom of the roots. The goddess clapped her hands to gain their dazed attention. Mr. Silver wrapped his hands around the arms of the chair, coiled to spring.

"I take back my gifts," Goddess said. "You may do what you want with the rest of your lives. I do not care to kill you. I do not care for you at all anymore."

She held her palms out before her, her long bony fingers almost obscenely thin, like tree branches. The bones in her wrists pressed against her taut skin.

"You wretched whore—" Mr. Silver launched himself from his chair, but the bones split through the goddess's skin in ragged brown reeds. Before Mr. Silver could even fully stand, the jagged ends of the reeds plunged into his chest, knocking him back into his chair.

Mr. Black screamed, scrambling to get to his feet. Terra's collar bones grew out of her chest, long, peeling segments of cattail stems, burrowing into Black's throat.

"Great Goddess, please I beg of you! Spare me! I will grovel at your feet for all my days!" Mr. Black screamed as reeds burrowed into him.

Mr. Green forced himself to stay still. Small bones slid out of her fingertips, over the table and sliced into the veins of his wrists.

"Oh Goddess," he choked through his tears.

The reeds began to suck, pulling sharp, writhing, scraping pieces from every part of their bodies. Mr. Green's insides were ablaze with throbbing, slicing horror as the goddess emptied them of herself and all she had given them.

And all that they had taken.

Vincent, Georges, Yves, Jean-Michel, Dana…all their sparks that had fed these wretched roots within them were yanked from where they had nestled.

Mr. Green had already felt this pain. It was what they had done to their artists, the growing emptiness inside him. Jim, Kiki, and the other women watched with dull smiles as Goddess took back her gifts.

The goddess withdrew her needles, abruptly, the reeds sliding back beneath her skin. Her followers turned back to the TV and started chattering excitedly about characters, as if oblivious to the gasping cries of the men at the table before them. The puncture wounds at Mr. Green's wrists oozed a mud-colored liquid, then clotted and closed.

Goddess watched them a moment longer, her black eyes reflecting their agony back at them. At last, she blew a kiss and turned away. It seemed to jolt Mr. Silver and Mr. Black from their seats. They staggered, groaning, from the room and out of the brownstone.

Mr. Green remained, just trying to breathe.

"Why are you still here?" Goddess's irises shrunk down to a normal size again. "This is an important episode, and I've already missed a lot of it."

"Please—" Mr. Green's voice came out a crackling croak. He cleared his throat to try again. "Please, kill me now. I have failed you and all the artists I have found. I know the hell that awaits me, and I'd rather get on with it."

The goddess regarded him, her skin rippling around her thin lips as the last of her roots receding beneath her pale skin. "Gareth Vermeer. You came to this work honestly. You have a talent for recognizing talent but had no skills for bringing it to the world. Your grandfather, he got his day at last, did he not?"

"Two hundred years after his death," Mr. Green said. It was bittersweet to think of Opa, of the mission to see him recognized that first set young Gareth on a path toward that French swamp.

"Yes." The goddess nodded. "Do you still have that piece of his that he gave you? Or did you sell it?"

"I would never sell it," Mr. Green said with more indignation than he had the right to.

The goddess smiled. It was fully Terra Desmarais's smile. She had always been both things. "I will not kill you. I have let you keep what vitality you come by honestly. You will live out a mortal life and die a mortal death, and that is the time you have to make up for your cowardice and your greed. I grant you this privilege and not your partners, because you protected me when you thought I was helpless. You will have the rest of this lifetime to atone."

"Goddess, I do not want—"

"Shut up now." Terra barked, her eyes flashing with irritation. "We want to watch Arya."

She nodded toward the door and then turned her whole body away from him. Kiki nestled her head against Terra's shoulder and Terra planted a kiss on her temple. Suddenly they looked like any family, watching their show on a Sunday night.

Mr. Green's body shook as he pushed himself to his feet. He stumbled around the table, watching Terra. He wasn't sure what he wanted. For her to look at him again? For her to forgive him? What a ridiculous desire. She had already been so generous.

Yet he kept watching, as he staggered toward the door, kept hoping she would turn, she would smile that goofy crooked-tooth smile at him. He was sure when he walked out, he would never see her again.

He only got a look from Jim who raised his eyebrows and tapped the massive hammer that rested at his feet, as if to remind Green that he could murder him easily now. It was enough to motivate him into the hall.

This Fifth Avenue brownstone was their joined property, built for them in 1872, when the associates had arrived in New York for the first time. Its halls were adorned with the art collected over many lifetimes. As Garret Green forced one trembling foot in front of the other toward the marble arched door, he felt the hall pressing in around him. All this beauty, all these things, at the cost of his soul.

He would spend whatever time he had left atoning.

But first he needed to sleep for a week or a month or whatever it was normal people slept for.

24

Blood was spattered with the paint in Terra Desmarais's studio. Cedric stood in the master bedroom doorway for a long time, looking at it. Some of it was Bernard's. He was sure. The violence that went down in this room clung to the air, like a vapor, heavy, dark. Cedric waited for his body to react. To curl up into a ball and cry, or run screaming into the night.

When it didn't come, he went back to his studio, still clutching the perfume. He drank a bottle of very nice Riesling and worked until the dawn peered through his skylight windows. He slept for a solid eight hours then woke up and worked some more. He was making a series of mountain landscapes. In pinks and greens and purples.

He'd only ever been to the mountains two times when he was a kid, but he had recently recalled how beautiful they were and how much fun he'd had there with his family before everyone but his sister cut him off.

He called his sister, as he shoveled down take-out ramen for dinner, and they talked about things they hadn't talked about before. She invited him out to Lancaster, Pennsylvania, to stay for a week in her house surrounded by roses, and he agreed for the first time in years. She asked if she could tell their parents he would be there, and he said it was okay. Maybe they would come. Probably they wouldn't. But it didn't matter. He was infusing himself with stronger stuff.

Garret Green called Cedric while he was in Lancaster. Scott Silver had a sudden heart attack and died.

"Is Bernard okay?" Cedric asked.

"Cedric, Bernard has never been okay." Garret's voice was weak but heavy. "He and I will be at the funeral, if you want to come, but he will not ever love you the way you deserve to be loved."

Cedric caught a whiff of something strange and familiar in the air around him. "Will Terra be there?"

"Terra has left New York," Garret said. "I have a few of her pieces left to sell off and one she wanted me to give to you. But I don't expect she will be back. She and Jim were looking at villas in Italy."

"Lucky her," Cedric said, although the words sounded hollow.

"Indeed," Mr. Green said, his words just as empty.

Cedric ended up declining Mr. Silver's funeral. But asked about the studio he used that Mr. Silver had rented for him.

"He owned it," Mr. Green said. "Keep it."

Cedric wasn't sure how that worked, but he didn't argue.

A month later he got a text from Bernard.

Hey beautiful boy. I miss you.

Cedric didn't know why he went. It wasn't that Bernard had such a hold on him anymore. Ever since he'd heard him try to kidnap Terra Desmarais, Cedric had avoided the man he'd been so desperate for. Chasing unavailable men was apparently pretty common for children who had been rejected by their fathers. Cedric had recently learned that in therapy, and he wasn't anxious to fall back into the very bad habits he'd engaged in with Bernard.

Besides, he'd just started dating an investment banker, who was very cute. Cedric felt optimistic about this one. His sister liked him too.

But there was something desperate about Bernard's message, and so Cedric went to meet his former lover for dinner.

He recognized Bernard when he sat across from him, but barely. Bernard's dark good looks had shifted to gray and weathered. Heavy pouches hung beneath his dark eyes, and it was obvious by the unnatural matte of his hair that he had started to dye it.

"I got something for you." Bernard grinned, and the deepening lines around his mouth folded in a way that Cedric had never seen on him before. Bernard slipped a joint across the table.

"No thanks." Cedric slipped it back to him. He still smoked a little pot some evenings when he had an image he wanted to focus on, but he knew Bernard's drugs came laced with gaslight and manipulation. He found his curiosity was utterly satiated. He didn't accept another invitation from Bernard.

Garret Green remained his agent, and got him into some good galleries. When things got serious with the investment banker, Cedric surprised himself by putting a good chunk of his money into a nice house in Jersey for them. He was even more surprised by how much he liked the suburbs and gardening. A lot of bright pictures came from the first bloom of blue irises at their early eighties' colonial.

He got two invitations, a few months after he moved. One was to a gallery opening in South Carolina for Dana Glonciel.

I started painting sunflowers, and I can't stop, she wrote. *Anyway, people are crazy about them down here. They don't even know who I am, but they love these damned sunflowers, and I'm just happy to be painting something pretty. Hope you can come and see me.*

He and his fiancé marked the date on their calendar and scheduled the vacation.

The other was to a wedding of Mr. Garret Green and Ms. Sheena Meegan, at the Central Park Zoo. It was the first Cedric had even heard of the relationship, but it could only mean good business for him, even if his work mostly consisted of irises and tulips and his signature dark charcoal lines were becoming less and less his signature these days. He responded with a happy yes to the invitation.

That night he worked on a new piece, red tulips, and when he was almost finished, he slipped the blown glass perfume bottle out of the curio cabinet. He took it outside with him and lit up a small joint. Carefully he brought the bottle up to his face and sprayed the lightest spritz, breathing deep the timeless fragrance and remembering that in this vast universe he was merely a speck of light.

Someday the bottle would be empty.

Someday he may run out of ideas.

Someday all that he loved and all that he created would be dust.

It didn't matter.

For now, he made art.

muse

Acknowledgments

When I finished the first or second draft of this, sometime in that long, surreal year of 2020, I sent it to my mom. For most of my life she was my first reader, but for this story, she was also my expert in residence.

My mother was an accomplished artist and art teacher. My art teacher, in fact, which at times could make for some complications. I wonder if it is common for the children of teachers to never stop receiving lessons. There came a time when I put my own art aside, because I couldn't find my voice as my mother's student.

Stories were always my own creature, and my mother was always supportive of all creation. Although she had the tendency to bring light into all her work, she didn't shy away from the dark or the painful. She submitted my early stories to contests, and she encouraged me to go to college for creative writing.

She read my first novels and corrected my typos. My first editor. My first beta reader. My first audience.

It was also in 2020 that Mom told us that she was sick. What timing. She did the full treatment. Surgery, chemo, radiation. She lost her hair that she loved so much. Then it was done and she started recovering. Through it all she kept painting. Maybe more than ever. She burned with the kind of inspiration that comes when you are forced to stand on the edge of the abyss and confront your own mortality. Her work was abundant and brilliant.

Anyway, I sent her this story in September, 2020. She and I had often discussed the nature of inspiration, where ideas came from, how the art took on its own life at some point and it was less about creating it as it was directing it, like some unruly garden. She enjoyed the story and the characters, especially Cedric. She brought it up often afterwards, asking if I was trying to publish it.

Mom's illness crept back in last year. Mistakes were made.

I've written a hundred versions of this part but none of them have been right so I'm just going to blunder ahead.

I am angry with her and I am angrier at her doctors. I am so sad for her and for me and for my family.

It's tragic to lose someone at the end of a long struggle. I am in no way diminishing the grief that comes when you have finally reached the end.

But this wasn't supposed to be her end.

My mom checked into the hospital for pain management.

She died of heart failure three weeks later.

She wasn't done.

She wasn't ready.

We didn't expect it.

And I am angry. I don't know where to put this anger that spreads through me like blackened roots sometimes stabbing at the softest parts inside me and other times shooting out at the people around me.

But when the dust settled, I did know that I had to release this book that spoke so deeply to the desperate urge to create that she and I shared.

So this book is for her, first and foremost. She always was going to receive the dedication to my first book, but this one was the right one to give to her.

Thank you, Mommy. I miss you every day.

Now onto the nice parts.

I want to thank my publishing and editorial partners, River Eno and Susan Tulio. We've climbed a lot of this journey through writing and publishing together, and I could not have done it with anyone less kind, sharp and encouraging. As editors you helped me to make this mess into a book and comb my sometimes-erratic style into something meaningful, and as friends you have carried me through some very challenging times both personally and professional. As party people, though, you both truly are the most fun. Thank you, ladies. Spec Pub Besties 4 eva.

I want to thank my friend, William Donahue, who always seems to give much more than he takes and yet is still withholding his most recent work in progress from me after at least a year of asking. Bill, thank you for your expert eye, your keen understanding of horror and always your kindness. Now give me Mr. Papadoos.

Thank you, Chris Bauer, for the enthusiasm, support and literary images burned in my head that I'm not sure I can ever erase.

Natalie Dyen, who always has insightful suggestions and a ton of support, thank you.

Thank you, John Schoffstall, for always having the very specific notes or research I need.

Lucas Mangum for just writing some of the darkest horror I've ever read and showing me how it's done.

Melissa Sullivan for pushing me to get involved and finding the open doors.

Ef Deal for just being the best, all around.

And thank you to Nicole Sohanic, who helped guide me artistically when I was in dire need of direction.

To the esteemed Don Swaim, thank you for welcoming me into your community and demanding nothing less than constant growth. I have kicked most of my bad habits, alright? And to the other members of the BCWW who helped with this piece, Candace

Barrett, Beverly Black, Bob Cohen, Daniel Dorian, Jim Hamill, Jim Kempner, Wil Kirk, Fran Nadel, Jackie Nash, Ashara Shapiro, Alan Shils, Bill O'Toole and David Updike, working with you and receiving your unique insights has been a gift that I will draw from all my life.

I cannot leave out Renee, who has patiently read everything I sent her and let me pick her brain for hours over wine. And Chrissy for always having my back.

Last of all, thank you to Tom, Q and C. My hearts. Thank you just for being you, but not for asking me many questions while I'm actively typing. I love you.

If you are interested in check out the work of Patricia Allingham Carlson, or watching her lessons online

fineartamerica.com/profiles/patricia-allingham-carlson

On YouTube @patriciaallinghamcarlson

on Facebook @ The Art of Patricia Allingham Carlson

Art makes life worth living

Portrait of the Author
Daydreamer by Patricia Allingham Carlson

ABOUT THE AUTHOR

LCW Allingham (she/her) is a Philadelphia area author, artist, musician and editor. Her early education was uniquely rich in the arts, learning music, performance and fine art all of her life, but she was always compelled toward the written word and storytelling. She received her degree in Journalism from Temple University and wrote home renovation articles before turning her focus exclusively to fiction. Her short stories have appeared in numerous anthologies and publications and she is an editor for the *Collection of Utter Speculation* series.

In 2022 she co-founded the indie press, Speculation Publications, with her long-time editorial partners and serves as executive editor. She writes in many genres but particularly horror, fantasy, historical and speculative fiction. She is an active feminist and human rights advocate and lives in Pennsylvania with her family, her pets and her ever expanding art collection.

Muse is her debut horror novella, and her debut novel, *Lady*, will be out in September 2024.

LCW Allingham

www.lcwallingham.com

Find me
on Facebook, X, Bluesky, TikTok & Instagram

And at

Speculation Publications

Check out the Collections of Utter Speculation
The Lost Colony of Roanoke
The Jersey Devil
Lady in White
The Dancing Plague
Cry Baby Bridge

And our other Books
Incubate: a horror collection of feminine power
Work in Progress: Story Crafting Notebook
Beach Shorts
Yule

www.speculationpub.com